"So it's a date?"

"If by 'date' you mean a mutually agreed upon and strictly platonic social outing intended to cheer up my daughter, then yes."

JT didn't seem offended. In fact, his lips actually twitched as if he might…

Yowza. In their few exchanges, she'd never seen him truly smile. Now a grin transformed his whole face, making his memorable gray eyes bright with humor.

"It's a date," he repeated, giving her one last unreadable look before walking past to tell the kids that he'd see them next weekend.

Kenzie, her legs feeling unsteady, stood listening to her daughter's exultant whoop of delight and the door closing as JT left.

Had she just received a glimpse of the man he'd once been? Because, despite what she'd said about not forming attachments at Peachy Acres, she suspected she could very much enjoy getting to know *that* man.

Dear Reader,

Welcome back to THE STATE OF PARENTHOOD miniseries, Harlequin American Romance's celebration of parenthood and place. In this, our 25th year of publishing great books, we're delighted to bring you these heartwarming stories that sing the praises of the home state of six different authors, and share the many trials and delights of being a parent.

In *A Dad for Her Twins* by Tanya Michaels, Kenzie Green is not looking for a new man in her life—and her neighbor JT most certainly isn't looking for instant fatherhood. Despite their outlooks, they find themselves thrown together at the end of one steamy Atlanta summer—thanks to a bit of matchmaking by her well-meaning twins!

There are five other books in the series. We hope you didn't miss Tina Leonard's *Texas Lullaby* (June '08), *Smoky Mountain Reunion* by Lynnette Kent (July '08) or *Cowboy Dad* by Cathy McDavid (August '08). Next month watch for Margot Early's *Holding the Baby*, a story about a woman who is carrying a child for her sister…a sister who suddenly decides she no longer wants the baby. Watch for our final book in the series, *A Daddy for Christmas* by Laura Marie Altom, when we head west to Oklahoma for a family holiday story you'll never forget.

We hope these romantic stories inspire you to celebrate where you live—because any place you raise a child is home.

Wishing you happy reading,

Kathleen Scheibling
Senior Editor
Harlequin American Romance

A Dad for Her Twins

TANYA MICHAELS

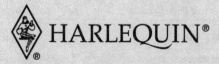

HARLEQUIN®

TORONTO • NEW YORK • LONDON
AMSTERDAM • PARIS • SYDNEY • HAMBURG
STOCKHOLM • ATHENS • TOKYO • MILAN • MADRID
PRAGUE • WARSAW • BUDAPEST • AUCKLAND

ISBN-13: 978-0-373-75229-4
ISBN-10:   0-373-75229-6

A DAD FOR HER TWINS

Printed in U.S.A.

ABOUT THE AUTHOR

Tanya Michaels started telling stories almost as soon as she could talk...and started stealing her mom's Harlequin romances less than a decade later. In 2003, Tanya was thrilled to have her first book, a romantic comedy, published by Harlequin Books. Since then, Tanya has sold nearly twenty books and is a two-time recipient of a Booksellers' Best Award, as well as a finalist for the Holt Medallion, National Readers' Choice Award and Romance Writers of America's prestigious RITA® Award. Tanya lives in Georgia with her husband, two preschoolers and an unpredictable cat, but you can visit Tanya online at www.tanyamichaels.com.

Books by Tanya Michaels

Don't miss any of our special offers. Write to us at the following address for information on our newest releases.

Harlequin Reader Service
U.S.: 3010 Walden Ave., P.O. Box 1325, Buffalo, NY 14269
Canadian: P.O. Box 609, Fort Erie, Ont. L2A 5X3

My heartfelt thanks to Kathleen Scheibling
for including me in the State of Parenthood series,
and all my love to Ryan and Hailey, even if
you do keep my life in a perpetual State of Chaos.

Chapter One

"Peachy Acres is a stupid name," Drew complained from the backseat.

Thank you, Mr. Optimism. Mackenzie Green, intrepid single mom and owner of a minivan that was older than her nine-year-old twins, sighed inwardly.

Kenzie empathized with her son's unhappiness over moving, but his negative commentary was making the four-hour trip from Raindrop, North Carolina, to Atlanta, Georgia, feel like an interminable cross-country trek. Or a voyage in space, she thought, vaguely recalling some old movie promo about no one being able to hear you scream. Too often Kenzie felt as if she were screaming on the inside.

Behind her, Leslie had adopted the prim, emphatic tone that made her sound like a cranky schoolteacher. "I'm sure it's called Peachy Acres because *Georgia* is the *Peach* State," she informed her brother.

Drew was unimpressed. "Know-it-all. I hate when you talk like you're older than me. We're the same age!"

"A person doesn't have to be *older* to be *smarter*."

"All right!" Kenzie took a breath, reminding herself that deep feelings of maternal love prevented her from strapping the kids to the roof for the duration of the trip. Well, maternal love and state laws. "You two be nice."

She was always a touch envious when she heard about inseparable twins who dressed alike and finished each other's sentences. It would be bliss if her children could just go a day without bickering. Heck, an *hour*—she wasn't picky! Tensions were running abnormally high today; the kids had said goodbye to the only home they'd ever known.

Leslie was coping by burying her nose in a young-adult reference book about Georgia during the Civil War, despite her increased tendency to get carsick while reading. Drew, as had become his habit this past spring, was channeling his misery into anger. Would the new setting do him good, giving him the chance for a fresh start and provide distractions like the zoo and natural-science museum, or were Kenzie's difficulties with her son about to get worse?

She'd debated turning down this transfer to a Georgia branch of the bank she worked for, but the Atlanta location had far more frequent job openings than the small bank in Raindrop, including the position of loan officer, to which she was being promoted. The stress of moving and the higher cost of living seemed worth the much-improved salary and increased odds of upward mobility. Another plus was that Kenzie's sister lived in the Atlanta area. Even if the two hadn't been close as children, it would do Kenzie and her kids some good to have family nearby. Nice, *stable* family.

Besides, although Kenzie was fond of the little town they'd been living in, she was looking forward to having the kids in a different school. She'd chosen their new home based largely on the district in which it was located. At the tiny elementary school in Raindrop, there had been no gifted curriculum to challenge bookish Leslie, and many of the instructors were a stone's throw from retirement. Drew's third-grade teacher, who had only a year left to go, had lacked the energy to address Drew's growing number of outbursts in class, countermanding Kenzie's warnings that losing his temper would carry consequences. Not that Kenzie blamed Mrs. Blaugarten for Drew's behavior problems.

While Drew had always been active, last spring had been the first time he'd taken his extracurricular sports seriously. He'd been surrounded by fathers coaching teams and volunteering to work the concession stands, dads coming to watch their sons score goals in soccer or hit a baseball into the outfield. For Drew, the runs he batted in paled in comparison to the fact his father had never witnessed them, despite glib promises to be there.

"Mo-om?" Leslie's plaintive wail cut through Kenzie's thoughts. "I don't feel so—"

"Pull over!" Drew yelled in a panicked voice. "She's gonna blow!"

Kenzie signaled with her blinker as Drew urged, "Hurry!"

Spoken like someone who's never tried to drive a minivan hauling a loaded trailer. She steered gently onto the shoulder, kicking herself for not insisting that Leslie put aside her books for once and sing along to the radio or, better yet, take a catnap to make the ride pass faster.

In the grassy ditch on the side of the road, Kenzie smoothed her daughter's blond hair and handed over a bottle of water from the minicooler in the front seat. Moments later, they were back on the road. Leslie was sufficiently recovered to start bickering with her brother again.

As she stemmed off the burgeoning argument, Kenzie met her own gaze in the rearview mirror. *Are we there yet?*

"KIDS? KIDS, WE'VE MADE it to Aunt Ann's street."

Both children had fallen asleep…during the final ten minutes of the drive. *Naturally.* Kenzie might have enjoyed the few moments of peace more if she weren't so tired herself. She'd been up at dawn to finish last-minute packing before getting the rental trailer this morning. After loading up their possessions and driving for hours, Kenzie's entire body ached.

Leslie lifted her head from its crooked angle against the seat and peered out the window. It was after seven but, due to the long summer days, still bright outside. Well-dressed children played on shiny scooters in driveways outside two-car, and even the occasional three-car, garages. The first time she'd been here, Kenzie had wrestled with twinges of resentment— who was she to question why the heck Ann and Forrest Smith needed a palatial, redbrick two-story to themselves? It wasn't *their* fault that Kenzie and the kids owned a secondhand couch with upholstery so garish it brought to mind the Las Vegas strip, or that they hadn't been able to afford replacing the dishwasher. Besides, Ann and Forrest had started a family now, so they'd probably grow into the space.

Kenzie was momentarily stymied as she approached the Smith residence. On the one hand, she didn't have enough experience maneuvering a trailer to comfortably navigate the driveway and the perfectly manicured flowering shrubs that lined it. On the other hand, she suspected the home owner's association governing the ritzy suburb had some sort of rule about staying parked in the street overnight. She pulled up to the curb for the time being and told herself she'd deal later with any uptight stipulations. The house she and the kids were buying on the opposite side of the city would be their first in an actual subdivision—with a name on the stone entrance and everything—but it didn't quite merit an HOA.

The front door to the house opened, and Kenzie's sister emerged. She'd been born Rhiannon, but these days she was

Ann, wife of an economics professor at a small but credentialed local college. Kenzie, twenty-eight and technically older by a year and a half, often felt like the younger sibling. Ann was always the one giving advice, accompanied by head-shaking and sighs. She'd been that way her entire life, determined that she knew better than her crazy parents and older sister.

It had taken until the twins' toddlerhood for Kenzie to realize that, however frustrating Ann's attitude over the years, her sister had a point. Witness how differently their lives had turned out.

Well, twenty-eight is hardly old, and this move is a new beginning. Kenzie had been making slow changes to her life for the past few years. This promotion gave her a chance to create a fresh start for her and the twins. From here on out, she would be practical Kenzie Green, loan officer and suburbanite.

With help from Ann on the legwork, Kenzie had found the perfect home. It wasn't a big house, but it came with like-new appliances, and the school system was fantastic. The only drawback was that the sellers, who were moving out of the country, had put the house up early in case it took time to get an offer. They didn't want to close until mid-October; Kenzie's job started next week. Hence, the Peachy Acres apartment complex and the short-term lease Kenzie had signed. Ann had made halfhearted noises about offering her guest rooms for the interim, but even her sister's spacious home would feel unbearably cramped by the time nearly three months passed.

Besides, living out here would create complications once school started, and involve a hellish commute. The apartment building, closer to the city, was just inside the edge of the kids' new school district. By staying at Peachy Acres until their house was ready, the twins could get settled into their classes and start making local friends. There was no way Kenzie was going to move them from Raindrop, enroll them in school near Ann's, then ask them to transfer *again,* later in the fall. She had assured her sister that letting them stay tonight was assistance enough.

"We were starting to worry!" Ann said from the driveway. "We expected you earlier."

Kenzie stretched, rubbing one palm against her lower back. "I'd planned to be here sooner, but you know how effective plans are once kids are involved."

Ann tilted her head, regarding her blankly.

What, baby Abigail never disrupted plans? Okay, that just wasn't fair.

It wasn't that Kenzie wished her sister ill, but when Kenzie had been a mother for five months, she'd been a sleep-deprived neurotic mess whose shirt was normally splattered in spit-up (Leslie's sensitive stomach had started from the cradle). Yet here was Ann, looking like an ad from a women's clothing catalog in her khaki capris, coral short-sleeved shirt and pearl earrings. Granted, she was plumper than she'd been before the baby, and Kenzie knew the pale blond bobbed hair was not her sister's natural color. Still, Ann was a vision of grace and loveliness.

Drew muscled between the two adults. "It took for-*e*-ver because Les here had to hurl every five minutes."

"I only got sick twice! *You're* the one who ordered the big soda at lunch and—"

"Kids!" Kenzie didn't yell, but her tone spoke volumes. If Leslie ever wanted another bookstore shopping spree or Drew planned to play another video game for the remainder of his natural life, they both needed to cease and desist.

"Well." Ann's green eyes were wide. "That certainly does sound like an eventful trip. Leslie, do you feel up to eating? I have a roast simmering. Forrest had hoped to join us for dinner, but he's teaching a weekly night course for the summer semester. He has a meeting in the morning, Kenzie, but he can help move big stuff in the afternoon."

"Roast beef? I'm starved!" Drew ran on ahead, food being his number one priority in a three-way tie with video games and sports.

"My stomach's fine now," Leslie said, "but I'm more interested in holding Abigail than eating."

"Maybe after dinner. She's taking her evening nap. I don't want to disturb her routine."

Kenzie stumbled as she stepped up onto the front porch. Ann had managed to instill a routine in a five-month-old? Amazing. Kenzie's recollection of the twins' first year was blurred, but they'd practically *never* slept…at least, not at the same time.

Should Kenzie seek her sister's parenting advice on how to deal with Drew's recent moodiness? Ann was certainly a solution-finder by nature. But any conversation about Drew's anger would inevitably lead to a discussion of Kenzie's ex-husband, Mick Green, absentee father and Aspiring Musician. He always talked about his dream as if it deserved capital letters.

Once, Mackenzie had been his biggest fan, a dewy-eyed teenager who just knew she was marrying the next Springsteen. *Mick and Mac—gag.* Looking back with adult hindsight, she would call their marriage the biggest mistake she'd ever made, except for one thing…well, two actually. Whatever else he'd failed to provide, Mick had given her the twins.

Even when Drew was glowering and Leslie was tossing her cookies, Kenzie loved them fiercely. The thought steadied her. Her little family could handle this transitional period.

Yesterday's mistakes had yielded today's blessings…and tomorrow stretched ahead of them, full of promise.

"NEED HELP?" The man addressing Kenzie had an intriguing voice—sort of low and growly, yet not unpleasant.

His tone, though, was laced with so much skepticism, as if she were *clearly* beyond help, that Kenzie wondered why he'd offered. Maybe it just seemed like the thing to do since she, a torn cardboard box and all of the box's former contents blocked his path. Her groan stemmed from equal parts embarrassment and sore muscles.

Glancing up from her sprawled position in the stairwell, she got her first good look at the potential knight in armor. Paint-stained denim and cotton, if you wanted to be literal, which she did. The new-and-improved practical Kenzie couldn't afford flights of fancy.

Then stop staring at this guy like he's the mystical embodiment of your fantasies.

Frankly, it had been too long since she'd had a decent fantasy, but if she had, it would look like him. Thick, dark hair, silver-gray eyes, strong jaw and broad, inviting shoulders. None of which were as relevant as her still being on her butt. She got to her feet…more or less.

As if she were having an out-of-body experience, she watched her wet sneaker slide across a piece of debris—the plaster head of a panda, she realized as she fell backward. The handsome stranger grabbed her elbow. Large hands, roughened skin. Since he was theoretically saving her from ignominious death in a dingy stairwell, she could forgive the lack of a delicate touch. The way her luck was running this morning, she would have broken her neck if he hadn't come along.

The man shook his head. "Lady." Was the undertone exasperation or amusement? Hard to tell from the single word.

"It's Kenzie," she said, grabbing the stair rail with both hands. "Kenzie Green. And thank you."

"No problem." He'd stepped back, either to keep from crushing her belongings under his work boots or simply to avoid her rain-soaked aura of doom.

She grimaced at the mess that covered half a dozen stairs. The coasters she was always admonishing the kids to use. Assorted books, her texts from some correspondence courses alongside Leslie's Mary Pope Osborne stories. Two mauve lamp shades. A statuette of a now-headless panda Kenzie had once received for donating to a wildlife fund, and various other small belongings that had been packed, taped up and neatly labeled Living Room in black marker.

"Guess they don't make cardboard boxes like they used to," she grumbled. What was wrong with the stupid box that it couldn't withstand being weakened with water and dropped down a few lousy steps?

Thank goodness Kenzie was such a levelheaded pragmatist. If she were given to the slightest bit of paranoia or superstition, she might see it as a bad sign that her first summer day in the sunny South was under deluge from a monsoon. She might be rethinking that rent check she'd written for a place where the elevator doors wouldn't even open.

"Are you the handyman?" she asked suddenly, taking in the man's clothing and an almost chemical smell she hadn't initially noticed. A cleaner of some kind, or paint? Maybe the elevator would be fixed before Ann arrived with the kids, not that Drew couldn't take three flights of stairs in a single breath. But he hardly needed new reasons to complain.

"The handyman?" Tall, Dark and Timely let out a bark of

laughter that was gone as soon it came. In fact, all traces of amusement disappeared from his expression so quickly she wondered if she'd imagined them.

"I'll take that as a no," she said. "It was an educated guess—Mr. Carlyle assured me that a handyman would be taking care of the elevators today. Which would make moving in a lot easier."

"Mr. C. *is* the handyman, in addition to being the property manager and the one who knocks on the doors whenever you're late with rent."

She stiffened. "I'm never late with rent."

He raised an eyebrow at her hostile tone. "I meant in general."

"Sorry. I take money seriously."

"You and everyone else." He grimaced absently, as if he were scowling at an unseen person. Did he owe someone money?

Oh, don't let him be one of those charming but perpetually broke deadbeats. There were too many of those in the world already. Then again, this guy wasn't technically all that charming. Hot, definitely, but not so much with the personality.

Imagining how Leslie would react to her mother calling a man *hot,* Kenzie grinned. "Well, thanks again. It was nice to almost meet you."

The corner of his lips quirked. "I'm JT. Good luck with the rest of your move." He started to pass, but stopped, watching as she wrestled with the lamp shades and books. With the box no longer intact, carting her belongings was problematic.

"I hate to impose," she began, "but were you in a hurry? It's going to take me a couple of trips to haul everything to the third floor, and if you wouldn't mind sticking around in the meantime to make sure no one…" What, stole her stuff? Who would want the book of *101 Jokes for Number-Crunchers* Drew got her last Christmas? "To make sure no one trips. I'd hate to be sued my first day in the city."

"I have a better idea." He was already sweeping up an armful of debris. After years of not having a guy in the household, it seemed bizarrely intimate to see this big man handle her possessions.

Books, Kenzie, not lingerie. Besides, people with better budgets than hers hired strangers to move their stuff all the time.

JT gestured toward the decapitated panda. "You keeping this poor fellow?"

"Sure. That's what they make glue for, right?" A couple of drops of that super all-stick compound and, as long as she managed not to chemically bond her fingers together, the panda should be as good as new.

Using the soggy cardboard in a way that reminded her of the baby sling she'd bought Ann, JT cradled the awkward bulk against his body. Between the two of them, they got it all up to her floor.

There were four units, two on each side of the hallway. Hers was the last on the left. As she unlocked her door, she heard JT's slight intake of breath, as if he were about to say something, but nothing followed. So she set down her load, turned to relieve him of his and thanked him one last time.

"I've got it from here," she said, hoping she sounded like a confident, self-sufficient woman.

"You sure?"

She thought about everything ahead—the new job, this temporary moving before the *real* move, trying to keep the kids from expiring of boredom until school started, and trying to keep them in their teachers' good graces once it did.

"Absolutely," she lied through her teeth. Next time she lectured the twins never to fib, she'd have to add the mental exception: *unless it's the only thing between you and a nervous breakdown.*

Chapter Two

"You're late." Sean Morrow glanced up from his lunch menu as JT took a seat on the other side of the table. With Sean's lean build, fair hair and expensive suit, the two men were a study in contrasts. "Dare I hope this means you were so caught up in a new painting that you lost track of time?"

"Actually, I was assisting a damsel in distress."

Sean pursed his lips, looking unsure about whether or not JT was kidding. "An attractive damsel?"

"Only if drenched waif is your type." To himself, JT admitted his words were a glib, incomplete assessment of Kenzie Green. *Good name.* Sounded like a vibrant, bright color—the kind he seldom used anymore—and it certainly rolled off the tongue more easily than *phthalo green* or *Antioch blue.*

Though Kenzie wouldn't necessarily turn men's heads on the street, she was put together with a grace of form that belied how they'd met. She was a slight woman with layers of burnished-gold hair that were probably a lighter honey when dry. Her deep blue eyes looked like the ocean when you were so far out the shore was no longer visible, and there was something geometrically appealing about her small face—

delicate blade of a nose, angular cheeks, an almost pugnaciously pointed chin that reminded him of some award-winning actress whose name eluded him. *Holly would have known.* Holly had been his link to pop culture.

She'd been his link to just about everything outside the studio, reminding him that there was a movie coming out he might like, reminding him of the names of acquaintances at openings, reminding him that he hadn't bothered to eat in nearly twelve hours. "How can I trust that you're going to help take care of this baby," she'd teased him once, "when you can't even remember to take care of yourself?"

Pregnancy had transformed her from the shyly smiling girl he'd first met to a laughing, excited woman with irrepressible humor. *I plan to decorate the nursery behind your back—I know you're the big-shot artist, but I'm scared you'll turn it into some abstract expression on spatial dynamics. I was thinking ducks and bunnies.*

"JT!" Sean's tone was pitched halfway between annoyance and concern. "Did you hear anything I said? You had that look again."

Stalling, JT sipped his water and tried to bring himself back to the present, a difficult feat given how much part of him longed to remain two years in the past. For the first few months after her death, thinking of Holly had hurt, creating electric shocks of pain that racked his whole being. Now that the sting had lessened, recalling cherished memories was comforting, beguiling. Easier than facing a future without her.

"It's hard," he said simply.

"I know." Sean lowered his gaze, a touch of sadness creeping into his own voice. "I know, man, but Holly wouldn't want you to be miserable. She would have wanted you to move on with your life. And she'd definitely want you to paint."

It wasn't as if he hadn't tried. The encaustic series he'd collaged in the weeks after the funeral—a sickening double funeral during which he'd felt he was putting his entire world into the ground—was his best work ever. But the frenzied creation of those paintings had hollowed him out somehow, leaving a void where inspiration had once been. He'd allowed Sean to hang the dark wax-and-oil images at the gallery, but couldn't bring himself to sell them.

The gallery. JT willed himself to focus. It wasn't fair that he left everything up to Sean these days; the two men were supposed to be equal business partners. JT was the one who knew art; Sean was gifted with people and finances.

Out of nowhere JT thought of the book he'd seen Kenzie holding—something about number crunching. Then there had been the reproachful set of her rosy mouth when she'd mentioned the importance of money. *I should introduce her to Sean.* Though the thought was mostly facetious, it certainly wouldn't be difficult to arrange. JT lived directly across the hall from his new neighbor.

"I've lost you again," Sean muttered.

"I was thinking about setting you up on a date."

"Seriously?" Sean grinned. "Not that I've ever needed help meeting ladies, but I take it as a good sign that you're thinking about *anyone's* love life."

"I'm not a monk," JT said defensively.

JT had gone on a half-dozen dates this year, but nothing lasting had come of them. It wasn't just that he missed Holly, it was more that he was still unsure of who he was without her. They'd met in Chicago when they were both college students. He'd become an adult during the years they'd been dating; he'd become a critically acclaimed artist during their marriage. He'd been about to become a father. With all of that taken away…

Since her death, JT had slept with only one woman, an art dealer Holly had liked and respected. In a bizarre way, JT had felt his late wife would approve. Marsha had been recovering from the shock of her husband walking out on her, needing to reaffirm her own feminine attraction, and JT had craved the touch of another person to penetrate his isolation. Their affair had lasted less than a month before they parted amicably, each somewhat healthier for the encounter, but knowing they had no future together. Sean had hinted several times that JT needed more of a social life. Even Mrs. Sanchez, who lived on the second floor of Peachy Acres and had appointed herself JT's godmother, for lack of a better description, nagged that his apartment needed a woman's touch.

Thankfully, the waitress came to take their orders, which gave JT something to think about besides his inability to paint and unwillingness to date.

Would there come a day when he could once again consider painting a joy, not an obligation? Would he ever again view love as a blessing and not a dreaded danger?

Some of his best paintings had evolved from brushstrokes with no direction, just moving his arm intuitively and watching to see what evolved on the canvas. If he kept getting out of bed each morning and facing each day, one after another, would his life begin to take some kind of shape? He couldn't be certain. But in the absence of an actual plan, he supposed he'd find out.

KENZIE THROBBED everywhere—muscles she hadn't realized she possessed were angrily making their presence known. She had a ton of unpacking to do, but all she really wanted was a long, hot soak in the bathtub. There wasn't time, though. Ann had called from her cell phone to say she was en route with the kids and "backup brawn." Besides, Kenzie was scared to test the bathroom's hot water. If it, like the building's elevator, the ceiling fan in her bedroom and the stove's faulty pilot light, neglected to work, she might cry.

Reminding herself that those were all minor inconveniences easily fixed, Kenzie grabbed a bottle of water from the refrigerator. Heck, she'd already relit the pilot light herself, and the worrisome smell of gas had dissipated. She sat on the brown living-room carpet, a shade probably chosen because it wouldn't show stains. That could come in handy with two kids. When the knock sounded at her door, she wasn't sure her legs would cooperate enough for her to stand, but she managed. Just barely.

Instead of the relatives she'd expected, it was Mr. Carlyle, a short man of indeterminate age. His thick hair was the color of freshly fallen snow, unmitigated by gray, and he had exchanged the navy track suit he'd worn this morning for an Atlanta Braves T-shirt with jeans and a tool belt.

"Afternoon, Miss Green." He peered past her at the cardboard boxes stacked beyond. Her apartment looked like an elementary student's homage to Stonehenge. "You settling in okay?"

"More or less."

"I won't bother you long, just came up to tell you the elevator's working again."

Oh, happy day! She and Forrest would need to bring the mattresses up through the stairwell, but the elevator would make everything else easier. "That's wonderful news. Thanks, Mr. Carlyle."

"Just doin' my job—and call me Mr. C. Everyone in the building does."

It's what JT had called the man this morning. For a moment, it was on the tip of her tongue to ask the property manager about the handsome mystery man. She assumed JT lived here, but didn't know that for sure. What was his last name? Did he ever smile? She ignored the random thoughts, telling herself they stemmed from exhaustion. Normally she was too worried about taking care of her own household to be nosy about others.

Kenzie had just finished giving Mr. C. a rundown of small repairs needed in the apartment when the elevator at the end of the hall dinged. The doors parted, and a teeming mass of cranky humanity spilled forth. Blond Leslie and dark-haired Drew led the way, bickering and power walking, each apparently determined to reach their mother first. Behind them, Ann's infant daughter, Abigail, was screaming bloody murder in her car seat. As Ann approached, Kenzie saw two wet circles on the front of her sister's shirt and tried not to feel relieved that Ann looked harried for a change. With them was her husband, Forrest. At first glance, he seemed to be talking to himself, but Kenzie quickly realized that he was wearing an earpiece attached to his phone and was trying to set up a tee time.

Amidst the noise—perhaps because of it?—the door directly behind Mr. C. opened, giving Kenzie a clear view of the person framed in the doorway. *JT.*

JT lived in the apartment across from her?

Her eyes locked with his, but calls of "Mom! Mom!" broke the spell. She looked toward her two kids and, in her peripheral vision, saw JT quickly shut his door. No doubt he was hiding on the other side, thinking, *There goes the neighborhood.*

FROM THE TWO HOPELESS expressions aimed at Kenzie as she set paper plates on the coffee table, one would think the kids were being served their last meal.

She sat cross-legged on the floor on the opposite side—

tomorrow, she'd get around to assembling the white pine dinette set. "Guys, you know this is only temporary. Everything will get better soon."

"Easy for you to say," her son said morosely. "You'll meet new people at your job. How are *we* supposed to make friends this summer?"

Kenzie knew from asking Mr. Carlyle that, of the twelve units in the building, ten were currently occupied, including hers and Mr. C.'s, which was on the first floor. He'd said there were a few teenagers in the building and one toddler, but no other elementary-school-aged kids.

Drew heaved a dramatic sigh, sounding for a change just like his sister. "We'll practically be shut-ins until school starts!"

The twins had protested that they were too old for day care. Kenzie had grudgingly said they could stay here by themselves for the duration of summer break—with her coming home each day for lunch and Ann making habitual drop-ins to keep them on their toes. Yet even after they'd begged permission to stay alone, Drew managed to make it seem as if a form of torture was being inflicted on them.

"School starts in a few weeks," Kenzie told them. "It will be here before you know it!"

Leslie picked at the crust on her tuna fish sandwich. "I miss my friends."

After less than twenty-four hours? "North Carolina isn't far. We can visit sometimes. Once we move into the house, we'll invite Stacy to come stay for a weekend."

"What about Paul?" Drew demanded from around a bite of sandwich. He never let being depressed stand in the way of his appetite. In fact, if Leslie continued to ignore her own food, he'd probably ask if he could have it.

"Sure," Kenzie said. "We could invite Paul, too. *If* the two of you behave, and after we're all settled."

"You mean once we have furniture again?" Drew asked.

With a spring starting to poke through the ugly upholstery, their thrift-store couch hadn't been worth the trouble to move. At this precise moment, just about everything seemed like more trouble than it was worth. But, as she'd promised the kids, it would get better. She had a few more days before she was due at work; maybe they should check the budget and spend half a day on something fun.

"There's lots of cool stuff to do around Atlanta," she stated. "Stone Mountain, the aquarium downtown, the Coke Museum, a planetarium." When she received only halfhearted murmurs of agreement, she played her ace. "Six Flags?"

Leslie glanced up with shining blue eyes. "Really? You never let me go anywhere with roller coasters!"

"Well, it's not like we had any theme parks in Raindrop."

"You promise you'll take us?" Leslie asked skeptically.

"Yes, but I'll need to get my first paycheck before we go."

"At least that's something to look forward to," Drew allowed before his face fell again. "We may not have had roller coasters back home, but I could have spent the summer swimming at Paul's. What kind of apartment doesn't have a pool? I thought that was, like, standard."

Instead of a pool, there was a communal balcony area on the roof, complete with grill and a couple of lounge chairs, which spared her the arguments about the kids swimming unsupervised while she was at work, thank goodness. "This place isn't so bad. And it's the only three bedroom we could afford."

"Small bedrooms," Leslie muttered, joining her brother for a seat on the Whiny Train.

"You guys would rather I find a place where you can share a room?"

The twins exchanged looks of mutual horror, quickly chorused, "No, Mom," and went back to their sandwiches without further complaint.

Drew didn't speak again until he was finished. "Mom, can I ask you something?"

"Of course, sweetheart."

Leslie darted a glance at her brother, shaking her head emphatically. Uh-oh. Whatever was coming next, the twins had clearly discussed it already…and disagreed. *Big surprise.*

"What is it, you guys?"

Drew steadfastly refused to look at his sister, who was attempting to bore holes in his skull with her glare. "Did you let Dad know we were moving? Does he have a way of, I dunno, reaching us here?"

"Oh, honey." Kenzie's heart constricted into a tight fist. "I left a message at his last known phone number, but the person who lived there said she hadn't seen your father in weeks."

"Told you." Using her thumb, Leslie crushed a corn chip on her plate. "If he cared about seeing us, or even hearing from us, he'd make it easier to find him."

"You take that back!" Drew's features contorted in fury, but beneath the youthful rage, he looked achingly vulnerable. Kenzie wanted to pull him into her lap for the hug she knew he wouldn't accept. "Dad does care."

Leslie rolled her eyes. "You really are a dummy."

"Leslie Nicole! You can apologize to your brother or go to your room."

The girl stood, her posture defiant.

"Les…" Far from sounding angry now, Drew's tone was imploring. He wanted her to share his belief that their father loved and missed them and would make more time when he finally "hit it big." Drew was the one who still allowed himself to hope, and Kenzie thought that was why he was always the angriest when Mick let them down.

Leslie tried to feign indifference. When the subject came up, she informed people that she didn't miss her father and that they were better off without him. But Kenzie had heard Leslie sniffling behind closed doors after these declarations. Kenzie watched her daughter go now, wondering what was the best way to handle the situation. Which was more detrimental—verbally bashing her ex and disillusioning her kids, or allowing them fruitless hope?

"Dad will visit us again," Drew maintained. "Eventually."

They never knew when Mick would pop back into their lives. His sporadic phone calls usually came—at an inappropriate hour—from wherever his band was playing. Most years he managed to send small, truck-stop Christmas presents that his son treasured as if they were gold. Three times since the divorce was final he'd actually sent Kenzie cash. Mick Green wasn't an evil man, but he was unreliable, inconsistent and suffered tunnel vision, keeping his eye on an unlikely prize and clinging to a fantasy of what he wanted to be when he grew up. Just as he hadn't listened when she'd said the Jagger-nots might not be such a great name for his band, he'd resisted her suggestions over the years that maybe it was time to find a different way to earn a living. Preferably something that generated income.

Would it be best if he stopped contacting the kids altogether? Given the way Drew was looking at her now, his heart visible in his sapphire eyes, she couldn't bring herself to ask Mick to do that.

"He *could* visit," she finally conceded. "I think it's unlikely we'll see him soon, but you never know."

Kenzie had never found time for another man in her life—not that there'd been a huge selection of age-appropriate bachelors in Raindrop. If she ever dated again, it would be a steady, predictable man with no creative aspirations. Someone she could depend on.

In the meantime, she'd just keep depending on herself.

Chapter Three

Though JT routinely lost track of time, his stomach always growled right on schedule at six on Friday. Enchilada night, or possibly taco casserole. His doorbell buzzed at exactly the expected hour—you could set a clock by Mrs. Sanchez—and he crumpled the drawing he'd been working on, tossing it in the general vicinity of an overflowing wastebasket. *I should empty that.* Mrs. Sanchez would bust his chops about the mess.

He opened the door of the apartment. Roberta Sanchez, who'd raised four children and was approaching double that in grandkids, lived below him with her husband, a MARTA bus driver. When she'd first heard that a widower had moved into Peachy Acres, she'd shown up with a covered pot of chicken tortilla soup. Food had followed every Friday since, with flan on his birthday.

"*Buenas noches,* Jonathan." She marched toward his kitchen with a foil-wrapped glass pan.

"Nobody calls me that," he reminded her.

Over her shoulder, she hitched a dark eyebrow. "Are you calling me a nobody?"

"Of course not."

"Then shut up. Now be a good boy and find me a clean

spoon, if such a thing exists here. No wonder you are uninspired to create beauty, living in such disorganization! Have you painted at all this week?"

He rummaged through a drawer. "You sound like Sean."

"I sound nothing like that degenerate!" She sniffed. "You should have heard him flirting with my daughter Rosa in the elevator. It's inappropriate, the things he says to a married woman."

JT grinned inwardly, knowing full well that Mrs. Sanchez adored Sean, a feeling that was mutual even though Sean called her the Battle Ax.

She paused. "You're not expecting him, are you? Maybe I should have brought more."

He eyed the pan. "That would feed an entire dinner party. Is Enrique working the night shift? You could join me."

"If you want me to join you, you should clean up this pit first." Despite her words, she pulled two plates down from the cabinet. "I'll stay. The good Lord knows my company is as close as you'll get to a dinner party. You don't want to be a hermit, Jonathan."

"I'm doing my part to uphold the reclusive artist stereotype."

"To qualify as an artist, shouldn't you produce *art* of some kind?"

Touché. "Nag, nag, nag. It's a wonder your children haven't moved farther away."

She sniffed again, not dignifying his jibe with a response.

The Sanchez family was the kind of close-knit group neither JT nor Holly had ever possessed. Holly would have loved Mrs. Sanchez; initially, that had been why he'd put up with the older woman's intrusions. But she'd won him over with her drill-sergeant tone and twinkling dark eyes. She seemed to understand his loss without ever expressing the cloying pity that made him want to withdraw more. Plus her cooking was a little piece of pepper-laced heaven.

JT didn't have a kitchen table, merely three padded, high-backed stools pushed up to the counter. He cleared away a pile of junk mail and an empty pizza box to make room for them to eat. Mrs. Sanchez pulled a carton of milk out of the refrigerator, opened it and immediately grimaced.

"Jonathan, this milk is older than some of my grandchildren."

"An unfair comparison. You have grandkids born every ten minutes!" He said it lightly, but it was the Sanchez babies that had made him leave the rooftop Fourth of July picnic last month.

Roberta had browbeaten him into attending, but he hadn't been able to bear it for long. Just as he hadn't been able to bear the empty nursery in the house he'd shared with Holly. After all the work she'd put into it, wanting it to be perfect for their child, he couldn't bring himself to paint over a single duck or bunny. The crib he'd assembled sat obscenely empty, and a month after he'd lost his cherished wife and the daughter he'd never had a chance to know, he'd bent over the railing and finally cried, ugly hoarse sobs that felt as if they were splitting him in half. From the moment the doctors had given him the news at the hospital, throughout the memorial service, he'd been too shocked and disbelieving to truly cry. Once he had, instead of feeling better for having poured out some of the pain, he'd been pissed off at the senseless loss.

He'd locked himself in his studio, barely eating or sleeping, trying to purge his enraged grief with painting. When he'd finished the series, he'd been like a man coming out of a coma, disoriented and unsure of how much time had passed. He'd wandered through his own house like a ghost, stopping in the nursery—that bright, cheerful room where he'd wept until he wished he'd died with them. Then he'd walked straight to the phone and arranged to put the house on the market, not caring where he lived as long as it was elsewhere.

"Jonathan." Suddenly Mrs. Sanchez was there, touching his shoulder. "Sit down. Eat. You need sustenance." She blessed the food, with a little pause before saying amen and making the sign of the cross. Had she added an extra silent prayer on his behalf?

It was odd. The only child of a wealthy couple, JT hadn't felt guilty that he was "disappointing" his parents by not going to law school and following in his father's footsteps. The elder Trelauney stubbornly spoke of a father-son practice even though JT had no interest in becoming an attorney. Instead of wasting his time arguing, JT had simply continued painting, ignoring his father's scorn over the "pointless scribblings." *You're on the cusp of manhood, son. Act like it! You're not some finger-painting toddler.* Yet JT had refused to feel ashamed. Now, by not painting, he felt he was disappointing Sean and Mrs. Sanchez—people who were better to him than he deserved—and that bothered him far more than his family's disapproval ever had.

Though he wasn't particularly hungry, he forced himself to take a bite of the enchiladas and was immediately rewarded with a spicy blend of rich flavors. "This is really good."

"I believe you meant great."

"I believe I did."

She reached for her glass of water. "You are a good boy, Jonathan. Even if you are a slob."

He surprised them both with a genuine chuckle.

Mrs. Sanchez looked pleased by this progress. "Mr. C. tells me that someone has moved in across from you. I'm glad. It's too quiet up here, with 3A unoccupied and that flight attendant in 3B gone half the time."

JT thought of that moment yesterday when he'd heard a baby shrieking, and had flung open his door. He still didn't know exactly why he'd reacted that way or what he'd expected to find. Though there had been only a handful of people on a floor that was often deserted except for him, it had sounded as if a deafening mob had descended. He'd heard plaintive shouts of "Mom" clearly directed at Kenzie. Was the baby hers, too? He didn't think so, but he hadn't stuck around long enough to inquire.

He winced at the memory and turned to his dinner guest. "It looks like my quiet days are over. The new neighbor lady has kids. Two, maybe three."

"Two," Mrs. Sanchez confirmed. "I asked Mr. C. He also mentioned she has no husband."

Was Kenzie divorced? Widowed, like himself? Technically, the presence of kids didn't require a husband in the first place. Maybe she'd never been married. There could still be a serious boyfriend in the mix. JT experienced a funny twinge in his chest he didn't want to examine too closely.

Feeling that he was being watched, he jerked his head up and found Mrs. Sanchez studying him. He didn't like the speculative gleam in her eyes.

"No," he said automatically.

She blinked. "I don't know what you mean."

Deciding this was as good a time as any to take her advice about tidying up, he rose and went to the dishwasher.

"You told me she had kids," Mrs. Sanchez said. "So you've met them?"

"Just her. Briefly." Despite his attempt to sound dismissive, the memory was vivid.

Kenzie Green had looked like the wreck he felt like on most days, yet there'd been determination glinting in her eyes and an unmistakable lifting of her chin when she'd stood to regather her belongings. He'd had the impression that life had knocked her down before and she was resolved to get back on her feet as many times as necessary.

"Well," Mrs. Sanchez prompted. "What is she like?"

"I don't know. About your height, blondish. I didn't exchange life stories with her."

"No," Mrs. Sanchez said, her voice disconcertingly gentle. "You wouldn't have, would you?"

He stiffened. "If you're so curious about Kenzie, you could have taken *her* the enchiladas instead of knocking on my door." The churlishness in his tone reminded him of his self-important father, and JT flinched.

But Mrs. Sanchez held herself above his rudeness with reproachful aplomb. "I fully intend to take her a dish this weekend and welcome her. I thought it better not to show up on her doorstep her first day, when she might be feeling tired and overwhelmed. I hate to intrude," she added with a faintly challenging air.

JT walked her to the door. "We're lucky to have you in the building, Mrs. Sanchez."

"You certainly are."

He hesitated before saying goodbye, unsure how to ask what was on his mind without putting ideas in her head. Mrs. Sanchez herself had said that, if any of her grown daughters had been single when JT moved in, she would have sent her up to deliver the homemade soup. So far, for all her fussing that he needed a woman's touch in his life, she'd lacked a spare female to nudge his way, deeming the flight attendant down the hall too frequently absent. Now there was a seemingly available woman living less than two yards from his front door. Surely Mrs. Sanchez knew better than to…

"You weren't planning to mention me to her, were you?" he demanded, unable to help himself.

"Hasn't she already met you for herself? What possible reason could I have for bringing you into the conversation? Is she some sort of art critic?"

He rocked back on his heels. "You've been known to spout the opinion that I would benefit from female companionship."

"I've also said you should eat more regularly, clean up this disorderly pigsty and go back to painting. Why would I inflict *you* on some girl who is already burdened with raising two children alone? Jonathan, *mijo,* you're probably the last thing she needs."

He stole a glance over her shoulder at Kenzie's door and tried to take stock of what he could possibly offer any woman at this point in his life. "You're undoubtedly right."

ON SATURDAY AFTERNOON, Kenzie excused herself to go downstairs and check the mail. She wasn't expecting anything other than standard Dear Occupant fare, but she'd been going a little stir crazy in the apartment. The kids seemed louder than normal today, and she couldn't chuck them out into a backyard to play. Showing the resilience of youth, they were back in better spirits. During a televised Braves game the night before, Drew had allowed that maybe living in Atlanta could be kind of cool.

Punching the elevator button, Kenzie considered the evening ahead. Would their finances, currently stretched by moving expenses and utility deposits, allow dinner out and a movie? Maybe if they went to the movie first, taking advantage of matinee prices, and eschewed concessions, then drank tap water at dinner rather than paying for sodas… She reached the bottom floor and dug in her pocket for the small silver key

Mr. C. had given her. This was the first time she'd checked to make sure it worked.

She gathered the handful of mail, sorting through it in the elevator on her way back up. Coupons, catalogs, the bill that her cell phone company had thoughtfully forwarded so that she wouldn't miss this month's opportunity to pay them. One yellow envelope was addressed to Jonathan Trelauney. Previous occupant? When she noticed the "3C," she realized the mailman must have just dropped it in her slot by mistake.

Jonathan Trelauney must be JT. His full name sounded familiar, but after dealing with so many people through the bank, eventually all names caused her moments of déjà vu. She'd encountered nearly half a dozen account holders with her sister's name.

When she stepped off the elevator, Kenzie glanced at JT's envelope. She'd been unpacking all day and was dusty. Her hair was tidy, pulled back in the habitual French twist she favored for work, but she didn't have any makeup—

Oh, for pity's sake! Handing the man his misdirected mail does not require mascara and perfume. Did she even own perfume? She couldn't remember the last time she'd treated herself to anything more luxurious than scented body wash.

Annoyed with herself, she rapped on his door a bit more curtly than she'd intended. At first she wasn't sure anyone would answer, but then she heard footsteps on the other side. JT appeared in the doorway, unshaven and *shirtless!*

Kenzie had taken a breath as the door opened; now she choked on her own oxygen. It took all her discipline not to let her gaze dwell on his leanly muscled torso or the dusting of dark hair across his broad chest. "I…is this a bad time?"

He rubbed a hand across his face. "I was sleeping on the couch."

"Oh." It seemed like a practically sinful indulgence, snoozing smack-dab in the middle of the afternoon, but then he didn't have two kids bouncing around and a zillion boxes to unpack. "I didn't mean to disturb you."

He regarded her with heavy-lidded eyes. "Did you need something?"

"Just bringing you this. It was in my mailbox." Their fingers brushed when he took the envelope, and she told herself that such a platonic touch would ordinarily not make her light-headed. It was the proximity of all that naked skin making her heart flutter. He must have a naturally golden complexion. He wasn't pale, but his color didn't seem to come from a tan, either. And, good grief, was she staring again?

Because she *was* actually staring, she noticed a splotch of dark violet paint near his rib cage. Suddenly the name clicked. "Jonathan Trelauney! I know you. Of you, rather. You're an artist."

JT was startled by two things—three, truthfully, but he was trying to ignore the unexpected sensation that had washed through him when their hands met. He didn't think the reaction came from the fleeting contact so much as her expression. Something akin to desire had flared in her eyes, and it had rocked him. No woman had looked at him like that in a long time. Hormones aside, he'd been surprised that Kenzie had heard of him. While his work had been renowned in certain circles, he was hardly a household name. Second, the *way* she'd said "You're an artist" had been filled with horrified discovery. She might as well have pronounced "You're a leper."

He frowned. "Do you follow art?" It seemed the only logical conclusion for recognizing his name, yet didn't explain her negative reaction.

"No. My hippie parents follow art. I've absorbed a few

details here and there during the rare visit with them." Though she kept her voice matter-of-fact, disdain leaked into her expression. The warmth in her earlier gaze had cooled completely.

Hippie parents? "Ah. I see."

Her hands went to her hips. "Just what do you 'see'?"

"Your parents were artistic, touchy-feely types, and you—" he hazarded a guess "—rebelled by growing up to be ultraconservative."

Her burst of laughter caught him off guard. "Whatever you do, don't give up art for psychiatry, because you couldn't be more wrong. My younger sister, Ann, was the conservative in the family. *I* married a musician at eighteen."

He glanced at her baggy shirt, sensible sneakers and pulled back hair. "You married a musician?"

"Yeah. And by nineteen, I had two babies to feed and clothe, so I reevaluated certain lifestyle choices."

JT wished she looked cynical instead of vulnerable. He felt…well, he wasn't sure, but she was a virtual stranger. He shouldn't be required to *feel* anything on her behalf. If he'd been more awake when he answered the door, his normal barriers in place, he would have said thanks for the mail and dismissed her without further conversation.

He could always try that now. "Well, thanks for the—"

Behind her, the door to 3D opened, and two kids stuck their heads out, seeming surprised to see their mother talking to some shirtless dude across the hall.

"Mom!" This from the girl, who looked scandalized. The boy glared silently in JT's direction.

Kenzie didn't help matters, blushing as if she'd been caught in the midst of something illicit. "What are you guys doing out here?"

"We were worried about you." The daughter fisted her

hands on her hips. Mini-Kenzie. "You said you were going to run get the mail, then you didn't come back. For all we knew, the elevator was stuck between floors!"

The boy looked faintly disappointed. "I had this plan for prying the doors open. Who's he?"

"Kids, this is our across-the-hall neighbor, Jonathan Trelauney."

"JT," he told the children. "Nice to meet you."

"These are my twins," Kenzie said. "Drew and Leslie."

"Not the identical kind of twins," Drew interjected.

JT bit back a smile. "I noticed."

"Why aren't you wearing a shirt?" The boy's tone was thick with suspicion. "Doesn't your air conditioner work? If you're hot, it would be smart to wear shorts instead of jeans."

Kenzie's head whipped around as she shot her son a warning glance. "Use your manners, Drew."

"But, Mom, I was just—"

"Let's get back in our own apartment and leave Mr. Tre-launey alone."

Yes, JT thought with relief. Alone would be good. He attempted his goodbye again. "Well, thanks—"

The elevator ding sounded, reminding him that Mrs. Sanchez had said she would bring Kenzie food and an official welcome today.

"—forthemail," he blurted. Then he shoved his door closed.

He caught a glimpse of Kenzie's mouth falling open. She was probably taken aback by his rudeness. If she'd known he was saving her from possible matchmaking attempts, she might have appreciated his efforts. A moment later, there was another knock. JT, trying to learn from his mistakes, was slow to answer.

"It's Sean," his friend called from the hall. "I know you're home. I just saw you shut the door in some poor woman's face."

JT ushered him in. "Don't judge me. It's complicated. You want a beer? I could use a beer."

Sean, dapper in a button-down shirt and slacks, and making JT feel like the Wild Man of Borneo in comparison, frowned. "Do you even have beer in the apartment?"

"Um…no." On his wedding anniversary, back in February, JT had gotten stinking blind drunk. After that, the thought of booze had made him sick for months and he'd avoided keeping any around. "Can I get you some lemonade?"

"All right, but only one, I have to drive," Sean deadpanned. "Tell me about the hottie in the hall."

"You can't call Kenzie a hottie," JT objected as he pulled a pitcher out of the refrigerator. "She has two kids."

"The boy and girl? She doesn't look old enough to have kids that age."

JT recalled what she'd said about marrying as a teenager, but didn't share the information with his friend; it seemed like a violation of privacy. "Why exactly are you here? Please don't tell me it's to ask if I'm painting anything. I was up until dawn, sketching and mixing colors on a canvas until my vision blurred."

"About that." Sean squirmed, looking uncomfortable, which was worrisome. Sean rarely let anything discomfit him. "Now don't be mad."

Lemonade missed its destination, splashing on the counter rather than into a glass. JT narrowed his eyes. "What did you do?"

"I was thinking entirely of you," Sean said. "Well, mostly of you. Partially. We are business partners. Financially linked?"

"I'm aware. Cut to the chase."

Sean swallowed. "I accepted a commission for you."

"You *what?*"

"This older couple, the Owenbys, came into the gallery last

night. You'd like them. Real marine-life enthusiasts, big contributors to the aquarium—"

"Sean!"

"They saw the abstract seascape mural of yours in Tennessee and want to hire you to do a much smaller version for their home."

"No."

"I told them they could leave a down payment with me and that I'd work out the details with you. Think of me as your agent."

"Which you aren't!"

"Don't you even want to know how much they're paying?"

"You had no business accepting that check!" JT thundered. He'd contact them and tell them no. Sean would refund their money. That would be that.

"I'm trying to help." Sean had raised his voice, too. It was unlike him to show such blatant emotion, which made his angry insistence doubly effective. "In case you haven't noticed, you've bottomed out."

"Gee, that escaped my attention."

"JT, I'm the best friend you've got, so get your head out of your ass and think it over. This doesn't even require the creativity of having a new idea. All you have to do is duplicate what already exists."

Pathetic. People were really willing to pay him money for that?

He wondered absently what his checking account looked like these days. He'd been coasting on some previous investments, what he'd made on the house sale and his part of the gallery proceeds. Gallery earnings, according to what Sean told him at lunch the other day, had steadily dipped for the past quarter. God, he *was* pathetic. Sean essentially did all the work in what was supposed to be a joint venture, picking up JT's slack for two years. Shame burned in his gut.

Maybe this was a way for JT to step up to the plate. Skulking around his apartment and waiting for his next great idea hadn't netted results.

"I thought it would help get you back in the habit," Sean pressed. "Kick-start your artistic drive."

"Oh, well then, I'll just slap some blue squiggly lines on a canvas and we'll all be happy, won't we?" But JT's sarcasm had lost its venomous edge. If he revisited a former painting, might it help him recapture what painting had been like back when he actually had inspiration?

He would do the painting, but he was still infuriated by Sean's high-handed techniques. Infuriated that he'd been reduced to this. He took a swig of his lemonade and walked past Sean, carrying both glasses.

"Where are you going with those?"

JT didn't bother glancing back. "To my studio to see if I can find something toxic to mix into yours."

"So is that a yes?"

"You should leave before I change my mind."

The front door opened before JT even finished his sentence, followed by a muffled whoop of triumph from the hall. JT was alone with two glasses of lemonade and the sudden fear that the only thing more pathetic than repainting something he'd already done would be painting a version that sucked.

Then again, at this point, what did he have left to lose?

Chapter Four

"I don't know, Mom," Leslie said from the beanbag chair where she was rereading *The Trumpet of the Swan*. "It still looks crooked."

Kenzie paused at the top of her stepladder to shoot her daughter a mock glare. "She who decides she'd rather read than help does not get to offer criticism."

"Would you actually let us help?" Drew asked excitedly, temporarily forgetting his handheld video game. "I didn't think I was allowed to climb up there or use a hammer."

"Well," Kenzie said, backpedaling, "there are lots of other things you could be doing if you wanted to lend a hand. Like wiping the remaining cabinets and drawers with a wet paper towel so I can finish putting away kitchen stuff."

Drew scrunched up his nose. "Lame."

Lame, huh? Then she hated to think what it said about her that she'd experienced a thrill of heady satisfaction after applying shelf liner to the pantry and closets last night.

Her moment of triumph, though, hadn't held quite the *zing* as the visceral thrill that had shot through her body when she'd seen JT's naked chest. That had been a much different sensation. Even now she tingled at the memory, glancing down guiltily to make sure the kids didn't realize their mom was having premature hot flashes over the new neighbor. She fanned herself with the framed picture she held.

"Mom?"

She almost jumped—not the best reaction at the top of a ladder. "Yes, Drew?"

"Why are you even hanging all this stuff?" he asked. "You're just gonna have to take it down in a couple of months when we move again."

For a change, he didn't sound bitter about relocating, merely curious.

"It's true that we won't be here long, but I want us to be comfortable and happy in the meantime." She indicated the pictures she'd already nailed into place. "This stuff makes me happy."

It was amazing how far some family pictures on the wall and colorful hand towels in the kitchen could go toward making a place cheerful and inviting. Mr. Carlyle had told them that residents in this particular building were allowed to make more changes than most, in terms of knobs, light fixtures and even painting the walls. Tenants were simply required either to return their surroundings to their original condition when they left or to pay for management to do so. Her short time here wasn't worth such effort, but she found herself imagining the difference she could make in the small apartment. It was cozier than it had first seemed when the atmosphere had been permeated with crankiness and the odor of damp cardboard.

There was a single bathroom, unfortunately, but it only held the toilet and bathtub. They each had a mirrored vanity and small private sink in the corner of their rooms. Like a hotel, Drew had said. Leslie had been ecstatic to have counter space for her hair stuff and lip gloss, and that she didn't have to share with her brother.

Because she was hammering a nail into the wall, Kenzie didn't realize there was someone at the door until Drew pointed it out to her. Leslie looked up with mild surprise, having been too engrossed in her novel to notice the knocking, either.

"Coming!" Kenzie called, descending from the ladder.

"Do you think it's that tall man?" Leslie asked. "The one who lives across the hall?"

"JT? I doubt it. I expect it's Mr. C. He said he'd be over sometime this weekend to fix my ceiling fan," Kenzie said. "What made you think of JT?"

Leslie shrugged. "He seems weird. Opening and shutting his door yesterday without saying anything. Standing there with no shirt and messy hair today. Like this creepy professor I read about in a mystery once where—"

"Les, later, okay?" Kenzie didn't want to open the door while her daughter was cataloging what she perceived as JT's eccentricities after only two brief encounters. *My kid is either too quick to judge, or she's bizarrely perceptive.* After all, weren't a lot of artists known for being eccentric?

Like musicians.

She told herself that her potent physical reaction to JT earlier was just the unexpected shock of being that close to undressed male flesh, quite a rarity for her. If Kenzie ever dated again, it wouldn't be with a sleep-tousled artist sporting careless dabs of paint across his flat abdomen. No, she would take the smart route…someone like the attractive man in the shirt and slacks who'd appeared in the hallway just as JT fled into the recesses of his apartment with hardly a goodbye. *Les is right. He's a little weird.*

Luckily, not everyone in the building was mysterious, anti-social and averse to smiling. Kenzie opened the door to find a short, dark-haired woman beaming at her over the top of a foil-wrapped casserole dish.

"I'm Roberta Sanchez," the lady said in a faintly accented voice. "Welcome to Peachy Acres!"

"Thank you," Kenzie said, touched. The friendly gesture of hospitality reminded her of Raindrop; she hadn't necessarily expected to find it so close to the heart of a city. "Please come in. I'm Kenzie Green, and these are my kids, Drew and Leslie."

Drew sniffed the air like a hound. "What kind of food did you bring?" he demanded.

"Drew, don't be rude." The way her son acted, people probably thought Kenzie habitually starved him.

"How was I rude?" He rolled his eyes. "Don't you think she wants us to be interested in whatever she made?"

Mrs. Sanchez gave him a look that convinced Kenzie the older woman had children of her own. "Regardless, you should not talk back to your mother." Then she smiled, lowering her voice to a conspiratorial whisper. "And it's tamale pie."

It smelled incredible, and Kenzie's stomach gurgled with appreciation. She'd been so caught up in the visual progress she was making in the apartment that she hadn't realized how close it was getting to dinnertime. And heaven knew that when Leslie was lost in a book, she didn't stop to eat or sleep unless prompted. *Oops.* In light of her sarcastic thoughts about Drew's appetite, she experienced a little pinch of guilt.

"So it's a dessert?" Drew asked.

"Different kind of pie." Kenzie took the warm pan from Mrs. Sanchez. Breathing in the scent of spiced meat and melted cheeses, she feared she might start drooling. "Leslie, say hello to our visitor." *Which doesn't mean a halfhearted wave without glancing up from the page,* she added with telepathic sternness.

Thankfully, the girl put the book down—after carefully saving her place with a bookmark bearing the wand-wielding image of Daniel Radcliffe. "Hi, I'm Leslie Green. You live in the building?"

Mrs. Sanchez nodded. "You'll love it here."

"We're not staying long," Drew said, his eyes locked on the dish in Kenzie's hand as he practically vibrated with the unspoken question, *When can we eat?*

"No?" Mrs. Sanchez looked crestfallen. "Oh, that's too bad. I already told some of my grandchildren that they might have kids to play with when they visited. And Jonathan—JT—could use some company. This floor is practically deserted."

"Are you sure he *wants* company?" Leslie asked. "He reminds me a little of this guy in a story who kept to himself and had crazy eyes. No one could prove anything, but the characters suspected—"

"Leslie! Why don't you find some plates? We should eat this wonderful-smelling tamale pie before it gets cold," Kenzie said. Drew bounded toward the kitchen, eager to assist if it meant eating soon.

Leslie was slower, heaving a sigh as she trudged after him. "No one *ever* wants to hear about my books. I thought parents were supposed to be *happy* when their children liked to read."

"Less attitude, more cooperation," Kenzie admonished. Then she turned back to Mrs. Sanchez, who was trying not to smile. "Sorry. They're not always like this." *Sometimes they're worse.*

"I understand. I raised four." The woman's gaze held both amusement and empathy. "You seem like you have your hands full. It's just you and the children?"

Kenzie nodded. "They don't see my ex on what you'd call a 'regular' basis."

Mrs. Sanchez clucked her tongue. Something about her

made Kenzie want to brew a pot of tea, sit down with the other woman and confide all her problems and doubts. Kenzie blinked, surprised by the impulse. She was accustomed to being self-sufficient. Her mother and father, bless their well-intentioned hearts, hadn't been big believers in hands-on parenting, afraid that too many guidelines and rules would "stifle" her individuality. So she'd made a lot of decisions from a young age…including the one to marry Mick.

Getting pregnant hadn't been a deliberate decision so much as a spontaneous celebration of a gig that was going to "put his band on the map." She'd never regretted having the twins, but once they were born, she had not only herself to look after but two small, dependent babies. Mick's failed attempts to be there for them had reinforced her determination to be independent. She must really be tired from the move if she was tempted to lean on a total stranger.

Straightening, Kenzie regained her composure. "Will you stay and eat with us, or do you have family waiting for you to join them for dinner?"

"Enrique and I ate early—he says waiting too late gives him heartburn at night—but I would love to stay for a few minutes and get to know you better."

Kenzie dished up three servings of the tamale pie and poured glasses of sweet tea. At her first bite of the dinner, she nearly moaned. "Oh, this is so good!" she told a delighted Mrs. Sanchez.

Drew grunted acknowledgment, but refused to slow his eating long enough to vocalize praise. Leslie looked disgusted by his behavior.

"Boys," she muttered imperiously. "Mrs. Sanchez, would you give my mom and me the recipe for this? We probably couldn't make it this good, but it might be fun to try."

"I'm pleased you like it!" Mrs. Sanchez said. "I'll bring the recipe up sometime this week."

"No practicing cooking while I'm at work, though," Kenzie told her daughter. "Sandwiches and microwaved snacks only." The kids were maturing, but not enough that she wanted them messing with a gas stove unsupervised.

When conversation revealed that Mrs. Sanchez was home most days, Kenzie thought about getting the woman's phone number so that the kids had an emergency contact right here in the building. Mrs. Sanchez seemed to know every one of their neighbors. Along with Mr. C., the first-floor tenants were a young married couple with a two-year-old who begged them to take her for rides on the elevator, a Georgia Tech grad student and the crusty Wilders.

"They've been married nearly forty years and have raised bickering to an art form," Mrs. Sanchez told Kenzie after the kids had cleared the table and returned to their abandoned book and video game. "They tell anyone who will listen that they're determined to outlive the other. If you ask me, though, they're crazy about each other and smart enough to know nobody else would put up with either of them."

The second floor, where Mrs. Sanchez and her husband lived, included a woman with six cats—Kenzie hated to think about her pet-deposit bill—and a family with two teenage daughters. Mrs. Sanchez said that should Kenzie ever need a sitter, she could give fifteen-year-old Alicia a call.

"Not her older sister, though. Boy crazy, that one. If she was thinking about a boy or on the phone with a boy—which she always is—she wouldn't notice a child spurting arterial blood in front of her. Then there's the third floor," Mrs. Sanchez continued. "You, a flight attendant named Meegan and, of course, Jonathan. You've met him?"

Kenzie nodded. Questions bubbled up inside her, trying to pop free, but she bit her tongue. Voicing any curiosity conflicted with her resolve as a practical single mother to have no interest in him.

Mrs. Sanchez paused, her prolonged silence and dark eyes making Kenzie feel as if she had to say *something*.

"He, uh, seems nice. We didn't talk much, but he helped me carry some stuff to the apartment when I dropped a box on the stairs."

"He's a good man," Mrs. Sanchez said, her tone wistful. "Sometimes, I wish I could have known him before…"

"Before what?" The question spilled out of its own volition. *Ann would be so disappointed.* Hadn't Kenzie, approaching thirty, learned to temper her impulses with more discipline?

To Kenzie's surprise, Mrs. Sanchez wasn't quick to fill in the blanks of JT's history as she had been with the other occupants.

"Before he moved here," was all she said. "He had a different life and must have been a very different man. Maybe you can get to know him better at the Labor Day rooftop picnic. Everyone in the building comes! Well, not Meegan, if she's traveling. You'll still be here Labor Day, won't you? That's right around the corner."

Kenzie nodded. "We don't move until mid-October. We just needed somewhere to stay in the interim."

"You picked the right place! Peachy Acres is a nice group of people, but a little nosy," Mrs. Sanchez said with a grin. "Once residents know I've met you, they'll want to hear all about the new lady in 3D."

"Not much to hear," Kenzie said. "Mother of two with a desk job at a bank. Very staid."

Mrs. Sanchez raised an eyebrow. "I suspect there is more to your story than that."

Not if I'm lucky. After her unorthodox childhood and tumultuous marriage, Kenzie aspired to an uneventful life with as few surprises as possible. Although, she conceded as she walked Mrs. Sanchez to the door and thanked her again for the unexpected visit and wonderful food, not all surprises were bad. As she had the thought, she couldn't help glancing past Mrs. Sanchez at the closed door of apartment 3C. Mrs. Sanchez's earlier words ran through her head. *He had a different life and must have been a very different man.*

What kind of surprises had life dealt Jonathan Trelauney?

IN ART SCHOOL, entire semesters could be spent in the study of perspective. There was no question JT needed to change *his* perspective. With a growl of frustration, he stood up from his desk. Maybe a change of scenery would help this afternoon. Sure as hell couldn't hurt.

In times past, he'd enjoyed the familiar scents of his workroom—the faint bite of oil, the sweet beeswax he sometimes worked with—but now he seemed to be suffocating on the stench of failure. Fresh air and a fresh outlook were definitely in order. *The roof.* He grabbed a sketch pad and a couple of charcoal pencils. Without allowing his gaze to linger on the door of Kenzie's apartment, he crossed the hall to the roof-access door, then took the stairs two at a time until he emerged into the brightness.

There was a lot to be said for natural light, but the sun overhead was nearly punishing in force. He was grateful for the rooftop breeze, even if it ruffled his pages and his hair. Impatiently pushing aside the dark strands that blew into his eyes, he tried to remember the last time he'd had a haircut. Sean had remarked that JT looked less civilized with each passing week.

JT had always been absentminded when it came to trivialities like regular haircuts—he'd been preoccupied creating his art. Now he was preoccupied with *not* creating it.

He settled himself in one of the chairs and scowled at the pencil in his hand, willing it to do something. Anything. After Sean's visit yesterday, JT had tried to work on the commissioned painting. How could he be stuck on something that was already finished? In theory, all he had to do was duplicate it— any halfway decent forger or first-year art student could do that.

The work needed something new, though, some flourish or detail or spin, otherwise the buyers weren't getting their money's worth, merely an adult version of paint-by-numbers. He'd tried throwing some paint on a canvas, playing, to see where it led…which was nowhere. Rather than continue to waste supplies, he thought he could sketch some ideas first. Finally his hand began moving, the pencil making a familiar soft scratching against the paper.

When it stopped, he stared at the thickly lettered sentence he'd written: *I am going to kill Sean.* Friend or not, the man had no business accepting a job on JT's behalf.

The sound of the metal door scraping across the concrete drew his attention. Kenzie's daughter stepped outside, blinking. When she saw him, she froze.

"You're that guy!"

He quirked an eyebrow. "And you're that kid who lives across from me."

"Leslie." She held a book in front of her, almost as though it were a tiny shield. "Mom said I could come up here to read."

There was little danger of anyone falling off the roof, with or without adult supervision, since the patio was surrounded by a tall mesh fence that slanted inward at the top. It was safe enough as long as the kid was wearing sunscreen, and all tenants had an equal right to be here. He gave her a gruff nod and hoped that she'd immerse herself in the book and leave him alone.

It took about two seconds for him to realize that wasn't going to happen.

"What are you doing up here?" she asked curiously.

"Working."

She didn't take the hint. "What kind of job do you have?"

"I paint."

"But you aren't painting now." She'd dropped her book on a chair and studied him, her expression imperious despite her diminutive status. Something in that moment reminded him of Holly, making him want to smile. "You don't even have paints with you."

JT ground his teeth. "I sketch ideas first, then paint later."

"Oh. Can I see what you're working on?" She was walking toward him as she voiced the rhetorical question.

"No, I—" He flipped the pad closed, but apparently not before she glimpsed some of the words.

"Kill Sean?" Her blue eyes were wide.

No doubt she'd tell Kenzie they were living across the hall from a homicidal maniac. "Don't ask. It's a long story." And none of her business, although that wasn't proving much of a deterrent.

She stiffened. "You think I wouldn't understand because I'm some dumb kid?"

"I—"

"Mrs. Griffin, our librarian, said she thought I was one of the smartest students in the whole elementary school!" Leslie's bottom lip trembled. Her indignation was morphing into something far more uncomfortable. "Now I won't get to see her *or* the teachers *or* the other kids in my class because we had to *move*. I wanted to stay in Raindrop!"

It wasn't his place to warn her that life often took unexpected directions. And it wasn't as if he could counsel her on weathering the bumps, since he hadn't recovered from his own. At a loss, he pointed toward her book, his tone abrupt in his own ears. "I thought you came up here to read. I'm trying to work here."

She burst into tears.

Oh, hell. He'd wanted to dissuade further conversation, but he hadn't meant to hurt her feelings. "Wait, I… No, don't do that. Please stop."

He stood, even though he had no idea what he planned to do. Go toward her? He couldn't reassure a little girl. What would he say—that everything would be all right? Yeah, that would be really convincing, coming from him. He could tell her that recent sleep deprivation made him a jackass, but that seemed inappropriate. Certainly his entreaty for her to stop hadn't accomplished anything.

Panic rose within him. What if she got more hysterical? Should he go get Kenzie? He winced, imagining what she'd do to him for reducing her kid to sobs.

"You're still crying," he said helplessly.

Oddly enough, that penetrated the girl's sniffles and fluttery gestures. She sent him a damp glare. "Thank you, Captain Obvious."

Her reaction surprised a chuckle out of him. "Aren't you too young for sarcasm?"

"No."

Well, all right then. What did he know about kids? He recalled his wife's excitement as she talked about their becoming parents. Would he have been a good father?

Leslie rubbed one eye, scowling at him with the other. "I wasn't crying because of you, just so you know."

"Oh. Good."

"It's just…I'm a pest. I should learn, being one of the smartest kids in Raindrop. I bothered my dad once when he was working on a song. He yelled at me."

What a jerk. Not that JT had done well himself, but shouldn't her actual father do a better job of relating?

"Sometimes I wonder if Drew and I weren't such pains, whether Dad would've stuck around. Then maybe we could have stayed in Raindrop. As a family."

Despite knowing that no one else was on the roof, JT reflexively looked around for help. The situation called for someone like Mrs. Sanchez or Sean, who always knew what to say to people. JT wished he were anywhere but here. This kid's home life was none of his business, and anything he said could potentially make her feel worse.

"I, ah…there are a lot of good things about Atlanta," he said awkwardly.

"Like what?"

"We have libraries here, just like they did in Raincloud."

"Raindrop." She sighed miserably. "But the libraries here won't have Mrs. Griffin, will they?"

"Eventually you'll miss it less," he mumbled.

"That doesn't help *now.*"

Her matter-of-fact statement was so true, he sent her an admiring glance. "You really are a smart kid."

"I know." Juxtaposed against the seeming arrogance in her words was the painful fragility in her expression. Her features were so much like her mother's that it was easy to picture the same vulnerability in Kenzie's eyes, although the mental image added to his discomfort. Did Kenzie know she was better off without her jerky ex, or did she—like her daughter—second-guess what went wrong and wonder if they'd made a mistake in coming to Atlanta?

"There's a great aquarium here," he said. "And some really good restaurants. Zoo Atlanta. Museums. I did a mural for a children's fine arts museum."

She looked skeptical a moment before allowing, "I guess you really are a painter."

"I really am." Or had been, once. "I even have VIP passes to the museum. I can bring guests in free of admission and stay for a little while after closing hours." Part of him recoiled in anticipation of the coming invitation. What was he doing, getting more involved with the Greens? Hadn't these few minutes on the roof been painful enough?

But he hated the expression in Leslie's eyes and his part in putting it there.

He never used his passes, and this kid was going through a rough time. Was he really such a heartless recluse that he couldn't spare a couple of hours to give her family a guided tour through a museum? Maybe he'd rediscover some inspiration while he was there.

"If your family's not already busy next weekend and your mom approves the idea, perhaps I could take the three of you to the museum for a little while, show you that Atlanta's not all bad?"

"For real?" Leslie's face brightened so suddenly she rivaled the sun. "That would be cool. Let's go ask Mom!"

"What, now?"

Nodding, she scooped up her book, then dashed toward the door. She shot a look over her shoulder, as if double-checking to make sure that he was coming. As if she was worried that, given the chance, he'd change his mind.

Yep, he thought with wry admiration. She was *definitely* a smart kid.

Chapter Five

Kenzie slid deeper into the vanilla-scented froth of bubbles, a sigh escaping her as heat seeped through her aching body. Oh, she needed this! Drew had just popped a movie into the DVD player, and Leslie was upstairs with a book. Was it possible Kenzie was about to enjoy an almost unheard of half hour of peace?

"Mom, Mom!"

You had to ask. She squeezed her eyes shut in denial, but called through the door, "What is it, Les?"

"I have to ask you something!"

"Can it wait, honey?"

Was it Kenzie's imagination, or did she hear the rumble of a lower voice out in the hallway? Her eyes opened. "Leslie, is Mr. Carlyle with you?"

"No. Mr. Trelauney."

Kenzie couldn't have grabbed for a towel any faster if her daughter had informed her that JT had X-ray vision. "Offer him a soda. I'll be out in a minute."

Sparing only a cursory wistful glance at the bathtub behind her, Kenzie hurriedly put on undergarments, followed by a faded polo shirt and a pair of denim shorts that got stuck on her damp thighs before obediently sliding into place. She looked disheveled, her hair curling in moist, frizzy ringlets about her shoulders, but at least she was dressed.

What was JT doing here? She doubted it was to bring them a neighborly casserole. Joining her daughter and neighbor in the kitchen, Kenzie was struck by how much smaller the room seemed when filled with JT's presence.

She swallowed. "Mr. Trelauney. To what do we owe the pleasure?"

Leslie bounced on the balls of her feet. "JT's gonna take us to a museum! Where he's a celebrity!"

"Let's not get ahead of ourselves, kid." The large artist looked comically uneasy next to her daughter—like a German shepherd afraid of a Chihuahua. He turned to Kenzie. "*Celebrity* is putting it too strongly, but I did some work for a museum that lets me bring guests. I told Leslie that we could *ask* about going some weekend…if you didn't mind."

"Please, Mom!" Leslie begged, looking more animated than she had since they'd first arrived in Atlanta. "I've read books about cool museums like the Louvre but I've never been to one. You said the good part about living here was all the stuff Raindrop didn't have. What do you think, Drew?"

He'd trailed his sister and their unexpected guest to the edge of the kitchen and stood against the wall, straightening just long enough to shrug his shoulders. "I'd rather go to a baseball game, but I guess a museum's okay."

"So can we, Mom?"

"Go watch the movie with Drew and let me discuss it with Mr. Trelauney."

"Okay. But he *wants* to take us. He invited us. You don't want to be rude to our new neighbor!"

Kenzie narrowed her eyes. "Out."

No sooner had Leslie gone than Kenzie wished she hadn't been so hasty. Now she was alone with JT, who looked just as good in a worn cotton T-shirt that lovingly molded his torso as he had without a shirt. *Really, Kenzie. You're a practical adult, not a hormone-stricken teen.*

"Can I get you that soft drink?" she offered.

"No, thanks. I don't want to impose."

"It seems my daughter was imposing on you. She didn't knock on your door, did she?" Maybe Kenzie should have paid more attention to whatever Les had been saying about the book with the reclusive man. If her daughter was bugging real people because of a fictional mystery, Kenzie needed to have a *long* talk with her.

"I was sketching up on the roof." He nodded toward a pad sitting on her kitchen counter. "She came up to read and started a conversation."

Figured. When Kenzie needed Leslie to do something, she couldn't draw the kid's attention out of a story. But when JT needed peace and quiet to do his work, her erstwhile bookworm turned into Chatty Cathy. "I'm sorry if she was bothering you."

He shuffled slightly, shifting his weight. "Our conversation didn't go very well."

"Define not very well."

"Adolescent-weeping unwell."

She frowned. "You made Leslie cry?"

"I was trying to work and suggested she read her book instead of bugging me. I didn't put it that bluntly," he added quickly, "but she started crying. Said something about bothering her dad when *he* was working."

"I see." She truly did. JT wasn't the one who'd hurt Leslie. That had been Mick.

Kenzie could hear her ex-husband in her head, snapping that if the kids weren't so distracting, he would have written a hit song by now. Of course, he'd apologized later. Mick always said he was sorry; that was his standard MO. What had changed was Kenzie's ability to accept the apologies.

"I'll talk to her," she said tiredly. "You don't have to take us on a field trip because you feel guilty."

"You'll probably be doing *me* the favor," he said, surprising her by not seizing the easy out. "Sean, my business partner, says I need to get out more. Maybe someone else's enthusiasm for art will help me reclaim my own."

"Artist's block?" she asked.

"Something like that."

Beneath his dry tone, there was a…vulnerability. She felt oddly drawn to him, this big man who seemed to shoulder even bigger problems. For a second she thought she might reach out, try to smooth his troubles away with a soft caress. *Stupid.* Jonathan Trelauney was not a little boy who needed nurturing. He was like Mick, a man at the whim of his "muse" or whatever. While other people toiled nine to five, JT moved restlessly through his days—or napped through them— seeking inspiration. If he'd snapped at Leslie upstairs, had it been out of frustration with Kenzie's daughter or simply frustration with himself and his artistic gift?

Déjà vu all over again.

"Mr. Trelauney, thank you for the invitation, but I really think it would be better if the kids and I don't join you." It was the same pleasant but inarguable tone she might have used when telling a bank customer that their loan had been declined. A touch apologetic but firm. JT would have to be obtuse not to get the message.

He moved toward her almost imperceptibly, not actually

taking a step but leaning as if to study her better. "You don't like me, do you?"

"I don't know you."

"And you don't want to." Strangely, he sounded almost amused.

Kenzie sighed. "Look, my kids and I are only going to be in the building for a brief time. We're waiting for our new house to be ready. So I probably won't get the chance to know anyone all that well. Don't take it personally."

"Go to the museum with me."

His persistence startled her. "Why are you pressing this? Given the way you practically slammed your door in my face when I brought your mail, I assumed you weren't interested in getting to know us, either."

Absently, he rubbed his knuckles over his stubbled jaw. "You're refreshing to be around. And a hell of a lot better than my own company."

What was she supposed to say to that? *Refreshing?* He made her sound like fruit juice.

"As you said," he continued, "you won't be here long. Why not take this short-lived opportunity to let an artist give Leslie a behind-the-scenes tour of a museum? It'll make her happy. She misses home, you know."

"Of course I know that!" In light of his valid point and obvious willingness to accompany them, it seemed churlish to continue refusing. "Fine."

His eyes widened in mild surprise. "So it's a date?"

"If by 'date' you mean a mutually agreed upon and strictly platonic social outing intended to cheer up my daughter, then yes." Her tone was so proper that Ann would have applauded. Deep down, Kenzie knew she sounded uptight, but this man did not bring out the best in her.

He didn't seem offended, though. In fact, his lips actually twitched, as if he might…

Yowza. In their few exchanges, she'd never seen him truly smile. Now a grin transformed his whole face, making his memorable gray eyes bright with humor. But the expression was fleeting, leaving the kitchen somehow a touch darker and dingier than it had been a moment ago. She had to fight the compulsion to cajole another smile from him.

"It's a date," he repeated, giving her one last unreadable look before walking past to tell the kids that he'd see them next weekend.

Kenzie, her legs feeling unsteady, listened to Leslie's exultant whoop of delight and to the door closing as JT left. Mrs. Sanchez had said she wished she'd known JT "before." Had Kenzie just received a glimpse at the man he'd once been? Because, despite what she'd said about not forming attachments at Peachy Acres, she suspected she could very much enjoy getting to know *that* man.

JT STRAIGHTENED, rolling his shoulders and blinking like a man waking from a dream—that's how painting had often felt to him, a kind of altered state of reality. Though he wasn't painting, at least he'd finally put something besides death threats against Sean on the pages of the damn sketch pad. Fidgeting with his pencil, he studied the image.

Not bad. He'd almost captured the play of emotions on the woman's face. Artistically speaking, this was better than anything he'd managed in weeks. On a personal level, however, he was a little disturbed to find himself sketching Kenzie Green at two in the morning.

He doubted she would appreciate being his subject.

Amazing how someone could be so prickly and so soft

at the same time. A study in contrasts. This afternoon, she'd tried to politely dissuade him from the museum visit. Despite a civil tone, there had been a chill in her gaze. Because he'd upset her daughter? Instead of being dissuaded, he'd stood there like a fool noticing that she smelled like vanilla, bringing to mind fresh-baked cookies warm from the oven.

Even hours later, he was still surprised that he'd pushed the museum invitation. After all, he'd only mentioned it to Leslie in the first place because he'd panicked at the sight of her tears…and had regretted the gesture nearly as quickly as he'd made it. He was not what Sean would call "a people person." What if they went to the museum on Saturday and it was an awkward disaster for all of them? What if he said something stupid and somehow made Leslie cry again?

Then Kenzie will knock your block off. Perversely, he found himself grinning at the prospect. He could tell she was a protective mama bear trying to do what was best for her cubs. And she was protective of herself. She handled it differently than he did, but it was there, a certain distance, an unspoken warning of "Don't get too close. I've been hurt."

He could empathize—sometimes he wasn't entirely comfortable being close to even Sean or Mrs. Sanchez. Unlike those two, Kenzie didn't know enough about him to pity him. There was no softened edge of sympathy in her dealings with him, and he appreciated that. He hadn't realized how much he *needed* that. Kenzie Green was too caught up in her small family and overcoming their obstacles to be worried about "poor JT."

With a sigh, he glanced back at the sketch.

He missed being an artist, missed the certainty of knowing who he was. And he was damn tired of being poor JT.

BARELY PAUSING in her phone conversation, Kenzie smiled and held up her index finger to signal that she'd be done in a moment. Ann nodded, choosing to stand while she waited. She fell into that unconscious sway that was habitual to many new mothers, keeping Abigail soothed inside her navy-and-white-checked baby sling. It was the first time she'd come inside Kenzie's new place of business, and Kenzie could see the approval on her sister's face. The marbleized floor spread from one end of the main lobby, where the tellers worked, to a row of judiciously spaced mahogany desks—one of which Kenzie now occupied—and beyond, to the offices reserved for those with seniority and supervisor positions.

When Kenzie was finished going over some interest rates with the customer, she bade the other woman a good day, slid off her headset and reached for the gold hoop earring she'd removed earlier. "I'm so glad you called," she told her sister. "I'm starving!"

"Buying you lunch seemed like the least I could do to help celebrate the new job. How'd your first week go?"

It was Thursday now, with the weekend—and her ill-advised "date" with JT—right around the corner. *Best not to think about that.* "Everyone here's great."

It wasn't Raindrop, where everyone knew her, but there was a certain relief in not being surrounded by colleagues who knew every detail of her life…such as what waitress Mick had spent the night with on his last visit to town. Her new co-workers seemed friendly, and her boss had three children of his own, which gave Kenzie hope that he'd understand when she had to leave early to pick up a sick kid or request a morning off for a school field trip.

Purse in hand, Kenzie rose. "So, what are we in the mood for?"

"Italian?" Ann asked hopefully. "We never eat it at home. Forrest says the acid in tomato sauce upsets his stomach, and Alfredo is too heavy."

"Sounds good to me," Kenzie said, wondering at the way her sister's mouth turned down when she said her husband's name. Ann could be opinionated, but she wasn't petty. If she was upset with Forrest about something, Kenzie doubted it was a lack of lasagna. "Everything okay?"

Ann blinked, her smile falling in place as automatically as if someone had flipped a switch. "Of course. What could possibly be wrong?"

In Ann's life? Good question. When Kenzie had been an impulsive teenager, she'd thought that her sister's approach of "thinking everything to death" was tedious and unimaginative. Time and circumstances had changed Kenzie's mind. If someone with Ann's discipline and organizational skills came into the bank for a loan, Kenzie would approve it instantly.

"What?" Ann asked, her smile replaced by a slightly more defensive expression. "You're looking at me funny. I told you, everything's okay."

"I believe you. I was just thinking that I'd like to be you when I grow up."

"Oh." Ann chuckled nervously, tucking a strand of hair behind her left ear. "Well, thank you."

They rode in Ann's car because it was outfitted with the baby's car seat, and Ann wound through several one-way streets, taking an indirect route to a small Italian café. She parallel parked with an ease Kenzie envied—*thank goodness we didn't bring the van*—and they climbed out onto the sidewalk. To the right of the front door was a patio enclosed with wrought-iron fencing and mostly shaded by a massive awning.

"You want to eat outside?" Kenzie asked. "Or will that be too hot for you and Abigail?"

"No, this is actually nice weather for August," Ann said. "You can almost tell fall is coming."

Fall. Kenzie thought ahead a few months, to the image of her Perfect House. She and the kids would be moved in by Halloween, trick-or-treating in their new neighborhood, officially starting a new life.

A dark-haired hostess with a wad of gum crammed in her cheek showed them to an outdoor table, and Kenzie watched her sister situate Abigail's carrier, raising the bonnet to offer further shade, and handing the baby a pre-prepared bottle. Looking back now, it was hard to believe Kenzie's own children had ever been this young. She'd been too preoccupied that first year with merely *surviving* to realize how little Mick contributed. It wasn't until much later that she'd started to come to her senses, and even then she'd been worried about whether she should have tried to make the marriage work for the children's sakes.

She was confident now that she'd made the right decision. Thinking of Drew's increasingly defiant expressions, she wondered how to convince her kids of that.

"So are the kids looking forward to school?" Ann asked once they'd ordered.

"Leslie is." School would be in session the week after next. "Drew's looking forward to finding out more about soccer leagues."

"Well, if they're looking to get out of the apartment in the meantime, y'all could come over this weekend," Ann offered. "We have that big community pool in the subdivision. Want to go swimming Saturday?"

Kenzie felt her cheeks warm and told herself it was the heat of the day. "Actually, the kids and I are going to an art museum on Saturday."

"Really? Which one? It's been awhile since I've been to the High," Ann mused. "Maybe I—"

"We're going as the guests of someone else," Kenzie blurted, afraid that her sister had been about to volunteer her company. Since she and Ann had never been very close growing up, it seemed odd that suddenly her sister was so omnipresent—babysitting the kids on Monday, so that Kenzie knew they were in good hands on her first day, then buying lunch today, and now wanting to get together Saturday. Did she want to make up for lost years? Was she simply doing her best to help them settle into a new city? Or…was Ann somehow lonely?

In theory, Kenzie wouldn't mind having her sister join in on the museum to help defray some of the awkwardness— *sexual tension*—between her and JT, but it didn't seem right to add members to their party without first asking him. Besides, Kenzie could just imagine how her sister and the eccentric artist would hit it off.

"Guests of someone else? You're making friends fast," Ann said with a smile. "Is this someone from the bank?"

Kenzie fidgeted in her seat, probably looking as guilty as Drew did when he was attempting a fib. "No. From Peachy Acres."

"That Mrs. Sanchez you told me about? She sounds lovely."

"She is. But no, not her." Kenzie scanned the patio, hoping for some sign of the waitress approaching with lunch. Maybe food would distract her sister.

"So?" Ann asked.

"So what?"

"Who invited you to the museum? You're acting awfully strange."

"I've always been the weird sister, right?" Kenzie forced a laugh.

Ann drummed her fingernails on the table.

"There's a guy in the building who was…is…an artist. He did some work for the museum, so he's giving us kind of a behind the scenes tour."

"Cool."

"Cool?" Hardly the reaction Kenzie had expected. "You're not going to grill me about who the guy is?"

"You just told me—he's a neighbor of yours and an artist." Ann studied her from beneath raised eyebrows. "Is there something else I need to know?"

When I see him, my heart beats faster. He's inspiring bubble-bath fantasies about acts my body forgot how to perform years ago. There's something about him that makes me want to share my feelings because I suspect he'd under-stand. "N-no. That's all there is to tell."

AFTER HER LUNCH WITH ANN, Kenzie managed to put her upcoming museum visit out of her head for the rest of the day. Friday passed quickly with high-volume business at the bank, and she was relieved to step into the lobby of Peachy Acres that evening. Mr. C. nodded to her on his way out, and she waited for the elevator, telling herself she should take the stairs for the exercise, but feeling too drained to motivate herself to do so. The doors parted with a ding and Sylvia Myer grinned at her over the top of her daughter's head.

"Afternoon, Kenzie."

"What number?" the little girl asked.

Sylvia shook her head. "I don't know why we ever spend money on toys. She'd be perfectly content to stay in the elevator all day."

They rode up to the third floor, and Kenzie could hear the muted thud of music as she approached her apartment. She'd worked out a nice deal with Alicia from downstairs, who came and "hung out" with the kids for the bulk of Kenzie's workday. While Drew and Les would have chafed at the idea of a babysitter, they didn't mind playing board games with a pretty high-school sophomore and listening to Jonas Brothers tunes while Kenzie navigated rush-hour traffic.

The thought of traffic made her grimace. Once they moved farther out to their Perfect House, her commute would lengthen considerably.

Behind her, JT's door creaked open and she jumped about a foot, her breath catching in her throat.

"Sorry, did I startle you?" a good-looking blond man asked, his tone both apologetic and amused as he stepped out into the hall and closed the door.

Sean, she recalled. They'd met briefly before. A nice guy and unrepentant flirt, according to Mrs. Sanchez. His light eyes were full of humor and easygoing charm, the opposite of the shadows that seemed to haunt his friend's gaze.

"I guess my mind was just somewhere else," she said, feeling foolish. "I don't know why I reacted like that."

He nodded, but pursed his lips in a thoughtful way that made her wonder if he'd guessed she was unnerved by the prospect of seeing JT. "I hear you're going to the children's art museum tomorrow."

Curiosity raced through her. What exactly had JT said about her and the twins? "Yeah, the kids are really looking forward to it."

Sean stepped closer, lowering his voice to a confidential tone. "I think the big guy is, too. Amazingly enough."

Although his words matched her initial surprise that JT hadn't graciously bowed out of the offer, she frowned. "Is it so amazing that an artist would enjoy a trip to an art museum?"

"Some days it's hard for him to enjoy much of anything."

Her pulse fluttered with a mixture of dread and excitement, as if she had inched closer to a secret she wasn't sure she wanted to discover. Would Sean fill in the blanks Mrs. Sanchez had left tantalizingly open? "He's been through a lot, hasn't he?"

He nodded. "Loss has a way of changing people. Be patient with him."

The implication of his words, combined with the intensity of his expression, rattled her. "Oh, but I— It's just a trip to the museum. For the kids. It's not like we're…"

"No?" Though Sean looked disappointed, he rallied quickly. "Sorry to have misread the situation."

"N-not at all," she stammered, more jittery than ever over tomorrow's date. *Get a grip. It hardly qualifies as a date when you're chaperoned by two nine-year-olds.*

Who was she kidding? Even if they were chaperoned by the entire student body of the kids' new elementary school, going somewhere with JT was the closest thing she'd had to a social life in years.

Chapter Six

"You should wear shorts, Mom. It's too hot out for jeans." Leslie sat on the edge of Kenzie's bed, watching her brush her hair in the vanity mirror. She had a book in her hands, but ignored it in favor of dispensing fashion advice. "Plus, you still have nice legs."

Kenzie smirked over her shoulder. "Be careful how you say *still*."

"Or a skirt," Leslie said with a snap of her fingers. "I'll bet Mr. Trelauney would like you in a skirt."

Alarm bells clanged in Kenzie's head. "Honey, I'm not dressing to impress Mr. Trelauney. This isn't a…romantic outing. I'm focusing on you and Drew and my new job for the foreseeable future. I don't have any interest in dating anyone."

Leslie flopped down dramatically on the mattress. "I'm *never* going to have a dad."

"You have a dad."

"Not really."

At times like this, Kenzie could cheerfully strangle her ex-husband. "I know your father doesn't get to see you as much as any of us would like, but he loves you and your brother."

When Leslie wrinkled her nose, saying nothing, Kenzie

moved to less dangerous territory and called out to her son. "Drew, we're leaving soon. Get your shoes on, please. And you'd better have paused that video game long enough to brush your hair."

He appeared in the doorway, scowling. "I can't find my other sneaker."

Before Kenzie could launch into an oft-repeated lecture about picking up after himself and staying organized, Leslie suggested, "Why not just wear your sandals? I saw them behind the couch."

"Thanks, Les." He turned to go.

"Tell Mom Mr. Trelauney would like her blue shirt," Leslie implored. "It brings out her eyes."

Looking back over his shoulder, Drew rolled his own eyes. "Mr. Trelauney's a guy. We don't notice that stuff."

"JT isn't a guy, he's a man. *Way* more mature than you. Plus, he's an artist, so of *course* he notices colors and composition."

Ann had taken the kids to a nearby library on Monday, and Leslie had been reading about art ever since. Motherly intuition told Kenzie they were on the cusp of Leslie's Next Big Phase.

The knock at their front door sent Drew scampering off for his sandals.

"I can answer it," Leslie told her mom, "if you want to finish getting ready."

Kenzie secured her hair in a simple twist and fastened the barrette clasp. "I am ready."

Still, she let Leslie hurry down the hall in front of her and open the door. Kenzie heard JT exchange greetings with the kids before she rounded the corner. Once she did, she froze in surprise.

The man smiling down at Leslie looked like a stranger, or at least an "after" JT, as if he'd participated in one of those makeover shows Leslie loved. JT had shaved since the last time Kenzie had seen him, and at first she thought he'd cut his hair, too. Upon closer inspection, she decided he'd simply tamed it into submission somehow. Gel, maybe? It wasn't slick or stiff. On the contrary, it looked entirely touchable. So much so that her fingertips tingled.

His clothes were notably different—wrinkle-free khaki slacks and a short-sleeved rayon shirt. The material was cranberry, with buttons down the front that were a shade or two brighter. It was conservative enough that he wouldn't have looked out of place in the bank, but different enough from his other clothes to make her realize that, for an artist, he didn't wear much color.

At that moment, he glanced up, his gaze colliding with hers. Her heartbeat stuttered, speeding up like an erratic recording before resuming its rhythm.

"Hi," she said, quickly breaking eye contact. "So… everyone ready to go? Shoes on the right feet, no one needs to hit the bathroom first?"

"Mo*ther!*" Leslie's face was a mask of mortification.

With a teasing glint in his silvery eyes, JT made a show of checking his shoes. "I think we're good."

Once they reached the parking garage, Drew asked if they could go in JT's car.

"Whatever you drive has to be cooler than Mom's minivan," he told the tall man. "Which one's yours?"

"That one." JT pointed toward a blue station wagon. It was in desperate need of being washed and didn't look much newer than Kenzie's van.

"A wagon?" Funny, she would have imagined him as the owner of a motorcycle or something.

"Got a good deal from its previous owner. It gets surprisingly good mileage and provided plenty of space for… my artwork," he said flatly.

The tension in his tone might be due to his lack of inspiration lately, but she suspected it was more than that. Not sure what to say, she simply offered, "I'll drive, you can navigate." Behind the wheel, she'd have a specific activity to accomplish and would feel less tongue-tied. She hoped.

Inside the van, Kenzie just barely refrained from reminding everyone to buckle their seat belts. She sighed inwardly, knowing that the twins wouldn't appreciate being mothered in front of JT, and that the man himself would probably be amused. *I was interesting once,* she thought wryly. Surely she'd held conversations that didn't involve reminding people to tie their laces before they tripped, or to take smaller bites so they didn't choke.

Yes, and where did being interesting get you? chided a voice that sounded a little like her sister's. Kenzie wouldn't trade her kids for the world, but she hadn't set out to be a single mom. It was a lot to shoulder alone, and at times she felt a twinge of guilt that maybe she wasn't providing everything they needed emotionally. Everything they'd get in a two-parent family that included a *reliable* father.

"Kenzie?" JT's husky voice captured her attention, sending shivers along her spine. "You heard what I said about turning left, didn't you?"

"Oh." She'd pulled up to the exit of the parking garage, then stalled out in her own thoughts. "Right. I mean left. I'm turning left now and heading toward Harris."

Kenzie didn't know why she'd been worried about any awkward silences. Leslie didn't allow any.

"I've been studying art all week," the girl told JT enthusiastically. "I didn't realize there were so many types! Just in painting there's impressionism, pointillism, abstract—"

"He knows," Drew interrupted. "*He's* an artist."

Though Kenzie glimpsed the resulting glare in the rearview mirror, Leslie continued as though her brother hadn't spoken. "So what kind of painting do you do, JT?"

"Mostly I work with oil, but also hot wax. Have you ever heard of encaustic painting?"

"No. It sounds fascinating."

Drew snorted.

JT swiveled around, his tone sympathetic. "Art isn't your cup of tea?"

Understatement of the year, Kenzie thought. Her son would probably just as soon throw himself from the moving automobile into oncoming traffic as sit trapped in the van for another half hour while his sister breathlessly peppered JT with painting questions.

"I like sports," Drew said, a note of challenge in his tone. He wasn't as easily won over as his sister.

"Sports are cool," JT agreed. "To watch, anyway. I was too uncoordinated to succeed in playing them."

"Hmm." Kenzie hadn't meant to make the small, puzzled sound. But truthfully, with his build and unthinking, almost negligent, grace she was surprised JT didn't have a more athletic background.

Not that she planned on saying exactly that, but given the quizzical way he was regarding her, she should say something. "I was just thinking you can't be any less coordinated than *me.* After all, you do remember how we met?"

In her peripheral vision, she saw his lips twitch.

"I'm great at sports," Drew said with all the modesty of a nine-year-old boy. "I play soccer and baseball. Too bad you didn't paint something useful like Turner Field, or we could be spending the day—"

"Andrew Green!" Kenzie was appalled at her son's rudeness. "Apologize immediately. And then I suggest that you sit quietly for the rest of the ride and think about how to be more respectful of other people and their varying interests."

"Sorry," Drew mumbled.

Great. They'd barely made it five blocks, and JT probably already regretted his invitation. This did not bode well for the rest of their day.

THE MUSEUM WAS DOING steady weekend business, but didn't seem jam-packed. There were a dozen or so people lined up in the gleaming lobby to purchase tickets. JT bypassed the main booth, crossing the hardwood floor toward the white counter on their left. The sign hanging above the counter read Members and VIP Parties.

A young woman with a blond ponytail and navy blazer glanced up with a smile. "Welcome to the Wilkes Fine Arts Youth Museum."

"Jonathan! Is that you?" A redhead in her thirties hurried to the end of the counter, flipping up a hinged section to join them on the other side. She stopped just shy of hugging JT, squeezing his arm instead. "It's great to see you."

"You, too, Beth."

"Been too long," she reprimanded him good-naturedly. "You know we'll issue you passes for any time you want to use them. Dare I hope you've been hidden away because you're working on a new series?"

"Beth, I'd like you to meet Kenzie Green and her kids, Drew and Leslie."

The redhead paused, then turned to include them in her bright smile. "Nice to meet you!"

Drew grunted a perfunctory hello. Leslie excitedly explained that this was their first visit and that she'd already mapped out online the exhibits she was most interested in. Meanwhile, Kenzie considered the other woman's body language. It was obvious Beth and JT shared some sort of history and that she cared about him. Was she attracted to him?

What woman wouldn't *be?*

Dangerous thought. Kenzie herself couldn't afford to be attracted. While the broody, mysterious loner type might cut a romantic figure in books or movies, in real life they didn't make good partners. In real life—if Kenzie ever risked depending on someone else again—she'd need someone staid who would patiently help Drew with math homework and remember to take the trash to the curb on the appropriate pickup day.

Of their own volition, her eyes stole toward JT again. As he talked to Beth, he allowed himself one of his rare smiles, and Kenzie's breath caught.

"Would you guys like to get started and investigate on your own," Beth asked, "or do you want me to personally give you the grand tour?"

"Thanks, but I'm going to play tour guide today," JT said.

Kenzie wouldn't have read anything into the refusal, but there was something just a bit too quick about the way he declined. Beth's first reaction was naked disappointment.

But she masked that and raised a quizzical brow instead. "Have fun," she told them all, sending JT one more searching look before ducking back behind the counter.

"What do you want to see first?" he asked the kids after handing them each a brochure with descriptions of the different areas and a rough map.

"Your mural," Leslie said loyally.

He chuckled, the sound rusty but endearing. "Suits me.

Then I don't have to worry about following some particularly brilliant piece of art. You guys want to take the elevator up a floor, or the stairs?"

"Stairs are good exercise," Kenzie blurted, thinking back to when they'd shared the elevator down to the parking garage, and her heightened awareness of him. He was just such a big man, he dominated any space he occupied. When a man that size embraced a woman, she must feel incomparably secure in his arms.

The kids, not quite but almost running, took the steps faster than the adults.

Lagging behind with JT, Kenzie heard herself comment, "Beth seems lovely—former flame?" *What are you* doing? *It's none of your business! You're supposed to be saving yourself for math-and-trash guy.*

"Actually, no. Former friend of my wife's."

"W-wife?" The unexpected word hit her in the midsection like a physical blow. It was a wonder she didn't tumble down the cement stairs in a reenacted parody of their first meeting.

"Late wife," he said softly.

"Oh." Her heart constricted.

The natural inclination when hearing about a person's loss was to apologize, yet Kenzie bit her tongue; he'd stiffened…almost as if bracing himself against the automatic response. Besides, Kenzie was still so stymied by the news that JT was a widower that she wasn't sure she could string together an intelligible sentence. Dozens of unanchored words roiled around her brain, colliding into one another and spinning into new questions and speculations. Had she just discovered the reason JT rarely smiled?

After a moment, it became clear neither one of them was going to say anything else. She felt ridiculously insensitive, meeting the news of his wife's death with nothing more than "oh," yet JT seemed to exude silent relief that they weren't going to discuss it. Maybe it was too painful for him. *Maybe he still loves her.*

"Are you two coming or what?" Drew called from the top of the stairs.

"Sorry," Kenzie said. "I slowed down for a sec to catch my breath."

Drew grumbled in a low mutter to his sister. Kenzie thought she made out the word *old*.

"He's not the most patient child in the world," she said to JT. "Deep down he's a sweet boy, but he's been… I want to apologize for what he said to you in the van."

JT turned toward her, his smile sardonic. "Don't worry, he's not the first person who didn't think my art was 'useful.' At least he has the excuse of being a kid."

She sucked in a breath at the hurt in his eyes.

He shook his head. "I was trying for humorous, but it came out bitter, didn't it?"

Wounded, she would have said.

"Suffice it to say," he continued in a more nonchalant tone, "my par—my father wasn't keen to have an artist for a son. Saw it as a foolish hobby to indulge and a waste of my potential. All behind me now. I just didn't want you to think my feelings are so easily bruised that I'd hold it against a nine-year-old boy that he'd rather be at a baseball game."

Ironically, that same boy now seemed eager to get started. "What is taking so long?" he demanded, a pleading note in his tone.

"We're on our way," JT called back, not glancing in Kenzie's direction as he took the stairs two at a time.

She was glad for the moment to collect her thoughts.

Whatever he might tell her—or himself—about having made his peace with his dad's disapproval, there was residual pain. Was JT so estranged from his parents that he hadn't been able to turn to them while coping with his wife's death? A sobering possibility. Much as she might wish in adult hindsight that her folks had raised her differently, with more structure, she'd never for a second questioned whether they loved her. She couldn't even fathom what heinous sin she'd have to commit to incur their disdain.

As a mother trying to do what was right by her own children, she experienced an immediate, albeit judgmental, flare of dislike for any father who alienated his son. Then again, was she being hypocritical? Did *she* respect JT's chosen career path, or did she also see it as wasted potential, a risky indulgence when there were monthly bills to pay? *Completely different circumstances.*

The benefit of not letting herself be romantically interested in a man like JT was avoiding those difficult dilemmas. She could merely be a distant but supportive friend, unworried by how his choices would affect her life or her kids'. It was best for all of them that he remain off-limits.

If only she could do a better job remembering that whenever a smile lit his eyes and his gaze warmed her skin.

Chapter Seven

"Wow! *You* did this?" Leslie asked over her shoulder.

JT almost smiled at her incredulity, which was simultaneously endearing and insulting. "Yep." He pointed at the initials slashed in deep purple at the bottom left corner.

The mural, a painting in bold colors of children playing at the Fountain of Rings in nearby Centennial Park, encompassed this entire section of wall. The kids in the picture were nearly as large as the two studying the work. Drew didn't share his sister's effusive enthusiasm, but he looked grudgingly impressed. At the very least, he didn't ask the kinds of questions JT might have expected: Why don't the kids have eyes or mouths? How come the sun is green? JT wouldn't describe himself as a Fauvist, but it was fair to say he'd been influenced by a Matisse exhibit his mother had taken him to see.

"This is really good." That hushed endorsement came from Kenzie.

Her praise affected him almost bodily, as if she'd reached out and stroked her hand along his bare skin. He couldn't help preening. Being an artist, neither could he resist asking what she liked about the work.

In response to being put on the spot, she glanced down, her

tone turning shyly hesitant. "It's a nice sense of…motion? Something about the way you've drawn the children seems so realistically active." A wry smile touched the corner of her mouth. "And trust me, I know active children."

He quirked his lips in wry acknowledgment. Her two kids had already moved on to a nearby enclosure that featured "junk art" laid out as floor sculpture.

Kenzie studied the mural in front of her, then looked at JT. Obviously she had other thoughts on the painting, but seemed reluctant to share them.

"What?" he prompted. "Is there something about it you don't like?" His voice was neutral, almost academic, as though he were an art professor coaxing a reaction from a promising student, even if JT felt more like a nervous teen trying to impress a first date. Good grief—were his palms actually turning damp? He'd been reviewed by some of the foremost art critics in the country, for crying out loud!

"Oh, no," Kenzie assured him. "I was serious when I said it was good. It's just, those vivid colors…"

When she trailed off apologetically, he knew she didn't plan to finish her sentence, but he could guess. Had she expected something starker? God knows he'd become less vibrant in the past couple of years—not that some of his darker work wasn't beautiful in its own right, but where had the colors gone? He'd tried once, experimentally, to force them, and the resulting canvas had struck him as garish and obscene. He didn't remember the joy of green suns and purple clouds or why neon pink had seemed the perfect color for a German shepherd.

Kenzie excused herself to check that her kids weren't touching anything they shouldn't be, and JT lingered at the mural. It was as much a picture of who he used to be as it was of children playing.

Holly would have been disappointed in him. She'd been too full of life to want him to fade into a colorless existence. Her potential disapproval from beyond the grave carried more weight than his father's cold disdain ever had. *I'll try harder,* he promised his late wife. He also knew she wouldn't have wanted him to be lonely, that she would have wished him happiness. Catching himself staring after Kenzie's retreating backside, he wondered if it was also time to try dating.

Maybe. But not with a skittish divorcee who had her own emotional baggage and two kids with father issues.

JT HAD NEVER VISITED an art venue with people who knew so little about art. As the day wore on, he found himself strangely charmed by the way Kenzie busied herself in the brochure and stammered whenever they encountered one of the many Do You Know…? stations located throughout the museum. Geared toward young guests, many of the trivia questions were intentionally easy, but it was clear she didn't have any of the answers. Even Leslie, who'd seemingly memorized half an art primer from the local library, had a full-fledged lightbulb moment, crying "Oh!" in the Impressionists' Hall when it dawned on her that Manet and Monet were not the same painter.

If Drew wasn't having the time of his life, he was at least participating in all the hands-on rooms that encouraged kids to put to work different principles of art. At the interactive display about sculpting, he went so far as to murmur "cool" before he caught himself. In contrast, Leslie was unabashedly getting a kick out of her day of culture and learning more about her newest interest. JT just wished Kenzie was having more fun.

Not that you did much to brighten her day.

What the hell was wrong with him? During their short acquaintance, he'd been thrilled she didn't feel sorry for him, so why had he blurted out two pieces of biographical information likely to evoke her pity? Though he'd never been particularly eloquent verbally, he couldn't believe he'd spoken so gracelessly about losing Holly. Yet when Kenzie has asked if Beth was a former flame, some part of him had wanted to make it immediately clear that she wasn't a romantic possibility…in the past or the present. Surely he hadn't been trying to reassure Kenzie that he was available?

He glanced to where she stood with Drew, discussing a piece of Colonial art and joking about life in pioneer days. Whenever her son had acted up today, forgetting his manners or talking too loudly, she was quick to correct him. Firm but fair. Once she'd addressed the problem, she let it go, resuming their conversations without holding a visible grudge. Whenever JT had disappointed his parents, the effects had been lasting. His mother had liked that he was more introspective than most boys his age. At the times he'd behaved in a more robust manner, she'd not only scolded him, but continued to send reproachful glances throughout the day, as if to remind him continuously that he'd let her down. And Jonathan, Sr.… Well, disappointing *him* was like inviting an arctic front, but without the snow to make it fun.

In JT's inexpert opinion, Kenzie had struck a nice balance with her parenting approach. He wondered if her kids knew how lucky they were. It was clear they missed their father and didn't see him often, but from what JT had pieced together, the man was selfishly temperamental. How did you explain to a pair of nine-year-olds that sometimes no father was better than a bad father?

As if feeling his gaze on her, Kenzie looked up suddenly, her eyes skittish.

"I, uh, was about to ask if you guys are getting hungry," he lied. "There's a café downstairs."

"Food!" Drew pumped a fist in the air, looking as excited as if they'd just offered him season's tickets to the Braves.

Kenzie ruffled her son's hair, a move that left him squirming. "All right, a lunch break sounds fine by me. Les?"

"Hmm?" The girl didn't even look up from the plaque she was reading.

"Earth to Leslie," Kenzie drawled. "Why don't we go eat, then maybe hit another exhibit or two before heading out?"

"Already?" Leslie squeaked with dismay.

"Soon." Kenzie darted a glance toward JT. "It was very nice of Mr. Trelauney to come with us, but we don't want to hold him hostage for the entire day."

JT started to insist that he was enjoying himself in his own understated way, but he hesitated. Kenzie wasn't entirely comfortable with him. Instead of working to put her at ease, perhaps he should be glad of the subtle emotional barrier between them. They took the stairwell down to the restaurant, and JT was careful to stay in front this time, ostensibly showing them the way, rather than lag behind alongside Kenzie.

For lunch, he and the kids ordered sandwiches and Kenzie grabbed a salad. The small café was furnished with round tables, ideal for solitary diners or couples, and larger booths along the wall. He wound up on a bench next to Leslie and directly across from her mother.

"Thank you for today," Kenzie told him as she drizzled dressing on her salad.

"Absolutely!" Leslie chirped. "It's been so much fun, hasn't it, Drew? The exhibits are great. I love the quotes on the ceilings, too. Man, even the food is good here."

Drew grunted. "How would you know? You won't shut up long enough to eat anything."

"Andrew, be nice to your sister! And don't talk with your mouth full."

"Yes, ma'am," he muttered.

Taking a bite of her sandwich with exaggerated precision, Leslie gave her brother a *so there* look, then immediately started talking again once she'd swallowed. "You know what other food is good, JT? My mom's cooking."

Kenzie chuckled. "I'm surprised you even remember what my cooking tastes like, between the sandwiches we've been eating recently and the dishes Mrs. Sanchez has brought over."

Drew made a sound that might have been a moan of ecstasy at the mention of Mrs. Sanchez's food; JT could relate. He grinned in the boy's direction, and Drew's expression immediately turned stony.

"Don't be silly, Mom. Of course I remember your cooking. Like your lasagna! Can you make it sometime soon?" Leslie swiveled on the seat and batted her eyelashes at JT. "Maybe you could join us. We usually have leftovers, so I'm sure it—"

"Leslie!"

JT wondered if Kenzie knew just how horrified she sounded.

Leslie stubbornly persisted. "What? He lives just across the hall, so it's not like he'd have to come out of his way. Drew, don't you think it would be a good idea for JT to join us for dinner sometime?"

At that, Drew's head jerked up from his sandwich. "No."

"Well, that's just rude," his sister said. "We owe him for today, and—"

"Not at all," JT tried to interject. "This was a favor with no strings attached."

"—*and* you talk about how you miss your friends back

home and can't wait to make new friends once school starts. What about Mom? *She* should have friends, too. Male friends," the girl said with significant emphasis.

Kenzie's face had turned a red so vivid it reminded JT of his earlier work. "Now, Leslie—" she began.

But it was Drew who jumped to his feet, shouting at his sister, "I can't believe you! Don't you love Dad at all? We can't just replace him with some painter who lives across the hall. Mom doesn't need 'male friends.' She has us. And Aunt Ann! Her dating is a *stupid* idea…even for you!" Then he stormed off toward the diner's exit.

For a split second, Kenzie was too stunned by her son's tantrum to react, but the shock quickly evaporated, leaving two very different emotions in its wake. Mortification almost nauseating in its intensity, and worry for her son, which eclipsed her personal embarrassment.

She rose, mumbling a half-formed apology as she turned to catch up with Drew. *It's getting worse.* His outbursts had steadily increased over the past year. She knew moving to Atlanta meant stressful change for the kids, but they were coping in very distinct ways. Leslie liked to lose herself in fantasy, whether through books or imagined romances between her mom and JT. Drew, on the other hand, simply seemed to be getting angrier. The twins had always had differences, but Kenzie couldn't believe the way he'd just screamed at his sister publicly.

"You owe Les an apology, you know," she said softly, reaching out to grab Drew's elbow before he could escape into the men's restroom. She led him toward a small bench between the water fountain and ATM machine. He didn't try to pull away, but he glared mutinously.

"Dating *is* a stupid idea," he reiterated. There was fire in his tone, but this was her baby—she didn't miss the way his lower lip trembled.

"For now, I agree. We have a lot on our plate, with my new job and school about to start. I'm not interested in finding a boyfriend. But worrying about that doesn't give you the right to be cruel to your sister."

His shoulders slumped. "Do you think after we move into the real house, you'll want a boyfriend?"

He looked so traumatized by the idea that she wanted to promise him that it would never happen. But that had been more Mick's style of parenting—saying whatever rash thing got him out of short-term trouble, with no thought toward long-range viability or consequences. "I honestly don't know, Drew. What I can tell you is that we'll work out whatever happens as a family."

Apparently *family* had been the wrong word to use, for he grew wild-eyed. "We've been here over a week. Has Dad even... There was this movie on cable where the kid found out his father had been writing him letters that his mom didn't want him to have."

Oh, Drew. His tone was so beseeching, begging her to lie to him and be the bad guy so that he could hang on to illusions about his father. "You know that's not the case, don't you?"

Saying nothing, he nodded, his eyes welling with tears.

His abject misery was almost paralyzing. The right words of comfort and wisdom just wouldn't come. Did other parents have this problem? Did the articulate moms and dads she'd known in Raindrop secretly get tongue-tied and insecure in the privacy of their own homes? She tried to channel warm but no-nonsense Mrs. Sanchez, whom she couldn't imagine ever shrinking from being candid with her kids. Maybe if Kenzie simply faked it, inspiration would strike.

But when she opened her mouth, all that emerged was a sigh. So she reached out and pulled Drew into a hug, hoping the wordless gesture said everything her son needed to hear.

In a change of plans not even Leslie protested, they left the museum right after lunch.

By tacit agreement, no one tried to make conversation on the way home. Instead they relied on the radio and let Star 94 gloss over the awkward silence. Thank God, Kenzie had decided to drive today. She had a foolproof excuse for staring straight ahead at the road and not even venturing a glance toward JT in the passenger seat.

What must the man think of her and her kids?

Kenzie eased the van into the parking space, and there was a small chorus of clicks and whooshes as her passengers unfastened their seat belts and let them snap back into place.

As he hopped out of the car, Drew asked over his shoulder, "Mom, is it okay with you if I take the stairs? Like you said, it's good exercise."

They both knew his request stemmed from embarrassment over what had happened earlier rather than dedication to physical fitness, but she saw no reason to humiliate him by making that point. "Sure. No running, though."

"Want me to go with you?" Leslie volunteered. It was an olive branch—she'd mostly ignored her brother since he'd yelled at her, and he smiled in relief and quick agreement.

They'd probably be arguing again before nightfall, but watching them walk away together, Kenzie was proud of them. Of course, this left her to share the elevator with JT.

"So," she began as the doors closed. "Eventful day, huh?"

The left corner of his lips twitched. "Don't take this the wrong way, but I'm exhausted."

"It would be hypocritical for me to take offense. I feel like exhaustion's been my natural state since they were born. But it's a good exhaustion," she added, not wanting to sound ungrateful for the two most important people in her life. "Fulfilling. Rewarding in a way that probably sounds ridiculous to someone with no children."

It was as if a dark cloud passed over his face, blotting out any sign of joy or teasing. His expression turned carefully blank. "Not at all. Paintings aren't kids, but many times I worked all night on a piece, found myself frustrated that I couldn't shape it the way I'd envisioned, later to accept that maybe it could be something even *more* than I'd imagined if I just had faith. So I'd slave away despite being tired, despite being exasperated, and when dawn broke and early sunlight spilled over what I accomplished, that's exactly what I felt— fulfilled. Rewarded."

Her breath hitched at the near poetry of his words. He spoke about his art with a passion that made her… Wincing, she reminded herself that Mick had spoken intently about his music, and that she'd once found his artistic dedication erotic, too.

"You were using the past tense," she noted. "Painting's not fulfilling anymore?"

"I wouldn't know."

The elevator lurched to a halt on the third floor, and as the doors slid open, Kenzie realized that someone sat in the hallway in front of her apartment. Not the twins, but her sister? A second look confirmed that it was indeed Ann and Abigail.

Along with several suitcases.

Chapter Eight

"Ann! Is everything okay?" Hurrying toward her, Kenzie temporarily forgot JT's presence behind her, until her sister's wide eyes reminded her. "Um, Ann, this is Jonathan Trelauney, the neighbor I told you about. JT, my sister."

"Nice to meet you." He glanced toward baby Abigail in her car seat, then looked away with a tight smile. "I'll just go so that you ladies can— Goodbye. Nice meeting you."

With his long-legged stride, he was across the hall and inside his own apartment within seconds.

Ann pursed her lips. "Odd. Really, really cute, though."

Yeah, that was JT in a nutshell. "What are you doing here? I mean, you're always welcome, but…"

Careful not to disturb the carrier in which Abigail was sleeping, Ann rose, stretching with a palm pressed to the small of her back. Sounding as casual as if she were asking Kenzie to pass cream for her coffee, she announced, "I've left Forrest."

And then she began crying, tears that had escalated to racking sobs by the time a startled Kenzie got the apartment unlocked. She ushered Ann inside, setting the baby on the coffee table in front of the new sofa. Kenzie was retrieving the luggage in the hall when the access door banged open and Drew and Leslie emerged.

Leslie drew up short. "What's all that?"

"Aunt Ann's bags. Your aunt may be staying with us for a couple of days," Kenzie guessed.

"Cool," Drew replied. "Think she'd make us some of that awesome roast beef while she's here?"

Kenzie rolled her eyes. "Baby Abigail is sleeping, so why don't the two of you tiptoe past and go watch something on the TV in my bedroom?"

Neither of them was terribly impressed with her television set, whose fuzzy resolution and limited color capabilities couldn't compete in today's Hi-Def world. They both nodded, though, and whispered brief hellos to Ann on their way through the front room. Kenzie was relieved to see her sister had managed to dam the tears. If the twins had paid better attention, they might have noticed that her eyes were swollen and her nose was red, but they were already engaged in a heated debate over what they should watch. Kenzie put the suitcases against the living room wall so that they were as out of the way as possible in the small room, then turned to her sister.

"Can I get you a cola? Wine?"

Ann's laugh was watery. "I'd take you up on that except I'm supposed to nurse Abby in the next half hour. I like a well-behaved baby, but I'm not trying to sedate her."

"Something else, then?"

"No, I'm fine."

"If you were fine," Kenzie pointed out gently, "I wouldn't find you sobbing in my hallway. By the way, didn't I give you the spare key?"

"Yes, but when I tried to reach you on the cell phone, it

rolled over to voice mail. It didn't seem right to just let myself into the apartment without your permission."

The matter-of-fact statement stung. Even if they hadn't been close during adolescence, it disturbed Kenzie that her little sister was more comfortable lingering in the hall like a vagrant than assuming she'd be welcome.

"Ann, please, my place is yours." She sat beside her on the couch, searching her sister's gaze. "Truly."

"I'm so glad you said that. Because I was…kind of hoping I could stay tonight. Maybe a couple."

"For as long as you need," Kenzie promised. She didn't want to pounce with dozens of questions, but her curiosity was a welling tide. What on earth could have possibly happened to prompt Ann to walk out on Forrest? *Do not tell me he had an affair.* If staid Forrest was making illicit whoopee, all hope for the male species was lost.

Blinking rapidly, as if trying to fan away tears before they had a chance to fall, Ann said, "I suppose you want to know what's going on?"

Yes! Preferably before her brain exploded from trying to puzzle through it. "Only if you want to tell me."

Ann tipped her head so that it rested atop the low-back sofa, addressing her response to the ceiling. "Do I look invisible to you? Am I invisible?"

"Of course not. Are you saying that Forrest's ignoring you?"

"Worse. If he just came home and didn't speak to me at all, I'd assume that he was preoccupied with something on campus. He knows I'm there. He comes right over to me every evening, gives me a perfunctory kiss right here—" she stabbed at her right cheek with her index finger "—and asks me what's for dinner. Usually without ever lifting his gaze from the day's mail as he sorts through envelopes. He doesn't ignore me in the strictest sense of the word, but he for damn sure doesn't *see* me."

Kenzie's mouth dropped open. She couldn't recall ever hearing her sister swear before. Though Kenzie could attest that if anything would urge you toward profanity, it was a failed marriage. This one didn't sound failed, however, merely in a rut. "It sucks that he's taking you for granted. Have you told him how you feel?"

Ann sat ramrod straight. "Ph.D. or no Ph.D., that—that *man* is an *idiot!* Last night I tried waiting for him at home in something a little more provocative than usual. Low-cut, with the perfume I thought he liked. He didn't notice. So when he got home from his Saturday class this afternoon, I tried talking. And he had the *nerve* to tell me it was postpartum hormones and that I was overreacting. *Do* you *think I'm overreacting?*"

Since the question was voiced in a slightly hysterical way that suggested homicidal retribution should Kenzie say yes, she quickly shook her head. "You sure I can't get you anything?" *Water, tissues, a mild tranquilizer?*

"I just need to feed Abby, then get some rest. I'm drained. Would you be affronted if I slept through dinner?"

Kenzie snorted. "What, and miss my four-star peanut butter sandwich?"

Reflexively, she thought of her daughter's claims earlier in the day about Kenzie's fabled cooking skills, and Leslie's attempt to have JT over. When Kenzie's undisciplined mind envisioned a dinner with their neighbor, the image didn't include peanut butter or children. Instead, her imagination conjured a candlelit meal, during which he would pour them each a glass of wine and forget to eat because he was staring at her in the soft illumination.

Shaking her head, Kenzie tried to dislodge the crazy fantasy.

While she was a reasonably attractive woman, she suspected she was past the age of being able to make men forsake sustenance. Besides, where were the twins in this daydream— at Ann's house? Unlikely, since Ann was here.

"Have you called Forrest?" Kenzie asked. "Just to let him know you're going to be staying with me, if nothing else?"

"Are you kidding? I left in tears and the big jerk didn't even bother calling my cell to make sure I was okay to drive. He can phone *me*...if he even notices the invisible girl is gone."

They should discuss this in more detail after Ann had had a chance to calm down. It was uncharacteristic for her to get so emotional, or to be critical of her steady husband. The fact that he'd been the kind of man who arrived home at exactly the same time every night and kissed her cheek in exactly the same spot had been what Ann loved about him. She'd been mature enough to admire predictability back when Kenzie had still thought relationships should be all about excitement and sparkle.

Well, I'm older and wiser now.

Pity, that. Because she suspected that JT, if it weren't for mourning his late wife, could provide enough sparkle to single-handedly simulate the Fourth of July.

ANN STAYED for the duration of the weekend, claiming it was no hassle for her to sleep on the couch, even though it wasn't a sofa bed. Despite her sister's Saturday rant about invisibility, Kenzie had assumed that by Sunday afternoon, Forrest would have come to collect his wife and daughter, and that Ann would miss her much bigger mattress and 300-thread-count sheets. Yet, as the kids' first day of school neared, Ann and baby Abigail were still ensconced in Kenzie's teeny apartment.

"You know," Ann said as she helped dry the plates after Monday night's dinner, "this place is surprisingly homey.

When we unloaded all your boxes here that first day, it didn't look like much."

Unpacking, hanging a few personal items, and the wafting scent of the enchilada casserole Mrs. Sanchez had brought when she heard Ann and baby were in residence did a lot to make the apartment cozy.

Kenzie glanced around, enjoying the rare approval from her sister. "Yeah, I did an okay job picking this, didn't I? Of course, luck had a lot to do with it." She'd been determined to find something affordable in the school district. Which reminded her... "Kids, you'd better be brushing your teeth! The first day of class might not be until Wednesday, but you need to get back in the habit of going to bed and getting up early."

Even from the hall, she could hear their groans. Once the twins were tucked in for the night, Ann asked if it would be all right to leave Abigail in her portable swing under Kenzie's supervision, and treat herself to a long bath.

"Take your time. There are bubbles on the shelf below the towels, if you want them." Kenzie turned on the electric swing. Soothed by its gentle metronomic sound, she stared into space and pondered her responsibilities as a sibling. Thinking aloud, she looked at the baby. "I'm her family. I'm supposed to interfere, right?"

Interfering hadn't been in either of her parents' nature, but Kenzie would bet everything she owned that Roberta Sanchez wouldn't hesitate to act if she felt it was in one of her relative's best interests. *I'm genuinely worried about Ann. I'm not doing this because I stubbed my toe on the portable crib while I was trying to leave for work this morning or because Abby cried— howled, really—from three in the morning to four.* Before she could talk herself out of it, she picked up the cordless phone from the coffee table and dialed.

It took several rings before Forrest answered the phone. "Hello?"

"This is Kenzie. Are you aware that your wife and daughter are staying with me?"

"Of course." He sounded vaguely baffled by the question.

"And are you planning to *do* anything about that?"

More bafflement. "Like what?"

Maybe Ann had been right and the man was an idiot. "Why haven't you called her?"

"Because I'm giving her space. That seemed like the patient thing to do. Ann is an eminently sensible woman. She's rarely overwrought. I wanted to give her time to sort through whatever issues she has. I'll be here for her when she's ready to come back."

Kenzie gritted her teeth. "Her 'issue' is that you don't pay enough attention to her! Now might be a good time to start."

"So you're saying she deliberately left in a manipulative bid for attention?" He sounded annoyed now.

Uh-oh. Why did Kenzie think she was the best person to assist with a marital spat when she was a divorcee who hadn't even kissed a guy since…since?

"Kenzie?"

"I'll let you get back to whatever you were doing."

"Before you go, can you ask Ann where my maroon tie with the royal-blue stripes is? I wanted to wear it to tomorrow's faculty meeting and can't seem to find it."

"You'll just have to make do, Forrest." Kenzie disconnected. Should she tell Ann about the attempt to help? She stole a guilty glance at the baby, who was watching in wide-eyed curiosity as she swung from left to right. "If it comes up in conversation with your mama, I will definitely tell her the truth."

But Ann seemed happy to avoid the subject of her marriage. When she came out of the bath, she asked if Kenzie wanted to watch a movie. "A chick flick! We could microwave some popcorn and stay up late."

Kenzie winced apologetically. "Actually, I think Drew ate the last of the popcorn. And I'm kind of pooped." She'd been working hard each day to get up to speed on her new job, coming in earlier than she had to and staying just a bit later on afternoons when Alicia or Ann was with the kids. Kenzie knew from experience that once school started, there would be myriad disruptions to her schedule, and she wanted to make a solid impression on the new boss before then.

"Oh." Ann glanced down, her hands twisting in the pockets of her robe. "Sorry, I was being selfish."

"No!" Kenzie got to her feet. "No, the truth is, I've been thinking about us. Our childhood. Our relationship. Now that we're both in Georgia, I hope that we can grow closer. Do more sisterly stuff."

"I'd like that. I know I was…bratty when we were younger. I was jealous, I guess."

"Of me?" Kenzie asked, startled. "I figured you were just mature beyond your years, and it took me awhile to catch up to you. Frankly, I've been struggling not to be jealous of *you*."

Ann's laugh sounded perilously close to a sob. "Why, because you've always had a secret yen to be the boring sister with the hollow accomplishments and inattentive husband?"

At least Ann still had a husband, while Kenzie's own marriage had disintegrated. "Ann, I know it's not exactly my business, but you and Forrest…"

"Yes?" She sat on the couch, her smile rueful. "Since I've invaded your home, I think you're entitled to an opinion."

But what was Kenzie's opinion? That it was better to be alone than with the wrong man? That good men who provided

well for their families were in short supply and after invest-
ing so much time and effort in her marriage, not to mention
the new baby, Ann owed it to herself to try to work things out
before walking away from Forrest for good? That while
Kenzie agreed Forrest could stand to be more affectionate,
pregnancy and birth *did* jumble a woman's hormones, and
being kissed on the same spot each day seemed like a dubious
reason for jilting a faithful husband?

"You know what? Never mind. I'm the last person you
should take advice from. I've only had one real relationship,
and even my fifteen-year-old sister could tell *that* was going
to be a disaster."

Ann flinched. "And I never let you forget it, did I? Man, I
was a know-it-all."

Kenzie hid a smile. At times, Leslie reminded her of a
young Ann. She loved both of them. "Okay, maybe you were
obnoxious about it at times, but you weren't wrong."

"No, but I was scared. You flung yourself into your
emotions. You experienced passion. I was always too afraid
to do that. I carefully planned my relationship with Forrest,
systematically seduced an older man. I mean, not necessarily in a sexual way. It was more of a domestic seduction. Now
I'm just…tired."

"Having a newborn in the house will do that to you,"
Kenzie sympathized.

"It's not Abby's fault. She's a darling. But *I* picked out her
pediatrician. *I* researched great preschools and already have her
on a waiting list. I plan what we're going to eat every night and
grocery shop accordingly. Hell, I practically lay out Forrest's
clothes for him! I don't want to be in charge anymore. At the
very least, I want to be a team, planning our life together. I want
spontaneity, which I know isn't his forte. He doesn't have to

sweep me off to Rome for the weekend, but maybe he could just call me around noon and say, 'Hey, instead of you cooking tonight, how 'bout I bring home a pizza?'"

Without meaning to, Kenzie laughed. "You don't ask much."

"I did," Ann corrected solemnly. "I asked for a perfect life. I demanded it, I created it. And now I'm not sure it's what I want. I wish, just once, that I'd done something wild and impetuous. That I'd been more like you. That my life was less khaki and more colorful."

Unbidden, the image of JT's mural rose in her mind, the bright swirls of color that created a high-energy picture of children having fun. It conveyed all the optimistic innocence of youth, when kids thought they were invincible and were content to draw neon-green moons and fluorescent-orange trees because they hadn't yet been told that they couldn't. Was that how JT had seen the world before his wife died?

"I guess none of us quite get the life we expected," Kenzie said softly. Thinking of her new job, the new school the kids were about to start and the Perfect House that awaited, she allowed herself hope, anyway. "Just because it wasn't what we imagined doesn't mean we can't find the beauty in it if we look."

Ann sniffed, considering. "I promise to keep my eyes open if you will."

"Deal."

"THIS IS GOOD." Sean blinked, moving away from the canvas to study it from another angle. "*Really* good."

JT chuckled tiredly. It was early evening on Wednesday and he'd barely slept more than two consecutive hours since Saturday. "Why does everyone always sound so damn surprised when they say that?"

Sean ignored the rhetorical question, still absorbed in the

painting JT had created for the Owenbys. "You mixed in some darker colors than the original."

If the first abstract was a picture of the sea, this one was the sea on a cloudy day. The same waters, but more turbulent. "The palette's not too bleak, is it?"

"No. No, the new shades add depth, texture."

There was another subtle change JT doubted anyone but him would notice. In the first painting, there had been scattered impressions of marine animals, such as clouds that were shaped vaguely like laughing dolphins if you looked at the right angle. For this version, he'd added a sea horse. Holly had laughingly told him in her third trimester that sea horses were her new favorite animal, since the *males* gave birth.

I would've traded places with you if I could've. But that had never been his decision to make, hadn't even been a possibility. What he did with his life now? That was his choice. Since he hadn't been able to sleep since the trip to the museum—plagued both by inappropriate dreams of Kenzie and the eerily muffled, almost phantom sound of a baby crying through the walls—he'd painted instead. If he hadn't experienced the same feverish joy of creation he'd once known, his grim determination had at least yielded results.

And he could breathe again. Wondering whether or not he'd ever finish another painting had become a stone weight across his lungs. Now, oxygen was slowly seeping back.

Sean clapped him on the shoulder. "I'm proud of you, man."

"Thanks." They stood for moment, silently acknowledging their bond of friendship and what it meant to each of them. "You ever accept another commission without talking to me, I'll kick your ass."

"Nah, I make it a point to stay in shape. I doubt you could take me. When was the last time you slept or ate? Or—" Sean sniffed delicately "—showered? Tell you what, I'll check scores on the tube while you clean up. Let me buy you dinner to celebrate."

JT's first impulse was to politely decline and stay holed up in his apartment to rest. But at the last second he stopped himself. "Okay." He'd been in hiding long enough.

ON WEDNESDAY AFTERNOON, Kenzie got permission to leave a smidge early—it had been the kids' first day of school and she wanted to hear all about it. More specifically, she wanted to hear that they'd liked their fellow students and had managed not to get into any trouble yet. As she pulled out of the bank's parking lot, her cell phone rang.

She noted that the call was coming from the apartment. "Hello?"

"Just me," Ann said cheerfully. "Kids got home safe."

"Thanks for letting me know." She'd walked them to the bus stop a few streets over that morning, threatening their lives if they didn't stay together on the way back in the afternoon. "I'm actually headed home now. Why don't we go out to dinner, and they can tell us all about their new classes?"

Ann laughed. "Sounds perfect to me…it was my night to cook."

Kenzie had to admit certain things had been easier with Ann pitching in to help, but she wondered how long she could offer her sister sanctuary without enabling her to hide from her problems.

By the time Kenzie made it through afternoon traffic and they had all three kids ready to go, it was nearly five-thirty. Waiting to lock the door, she was the last one out of her apartment—but the first to look up when the door across the hall opened. *JT.* Her heart skipped a beat in anticipation of seeing him. Somehow, despite their close living proximity, she'd avoided running into him since the weekend.

Disappointment so intense that it should have been comical hit when the man who emerged wasn't JT but his friend Sean.

"And who is this beautiful girl?" the man asked, smiling in Ann's direction.

"My sister," Kenzie replied. "My *married* sister." Apparently, twenty-eight was not too old for her protective big-sister instincts to kick in. Ann had recently admitted to wishing her life had included more passion; she might be vulnerable to the flirtatious attention of handsome strangers.

Sean glanced up with laughing eyes. "Actually, I meant the baby. Hi, Ann, I'm Sean, JT's friend and business partner. In fact, we were just headed out to dinner to celebrate his latest brilliant painting."

By now, JT had joined them in the hall. Dear heaven, he looked incredible. He wore a button-down black shirt with black jeans, and the monochromatic style was *really* working for him. His hair was damp and there was a gleam in his eyes that hadn't been there the last time they'd spoken. It gave him an irresistible edge of confidence.

Kenzie couldn't look away from him. "You've been painting? That's wonderful."

"Sean may be exaggerating the brilliance part," he said with a smile. "But it is pretty wonderful."

"We're going to dinner, too," Leslie said. "To celebrate the first day of school!"

"School isn't something to celebrate," Drew mumbled.

"Maybe we should all go togeth—"

"Leslie! I'm sure the men probably want to talk business and—"

"Not at all," Sean said smoothly. "I've been saying for

months that what the big guy needs is more fun in his life. I know a great place where we can get decent food and play, too."

Drew looked intrigued despite himself. "What kind of playing?"

Kenzie tried again, feeling that she was rapidly losing control of the situation. If she'd ever had any in the first place. "Oh, but it's a school night. The kids shouldn't be out too late."

"Then we should get going," Ann said cheerfully. "It's not even six yet. We have plenty of time."

What are you doing? Kenzie demanded with her narrow-eyed glare.

Her sister fussed with the straps of Abby's car seat and pretended not to notice.

Despite the objections she'd tried to voice, fifteen minutes later Kenzie parked next to Sean's black car at a restaurant that boasted an indoor miniature golf course, and hoped for the best.

Chapter Nine

"Welcome to Course After Course!" A bubbly hostess smiled at them. "How many in your party?"

"Four adults, two kids and one baby requiring a high chair," Ann said.

We're just missing the partridge and the pear tree. How, Kenzie wondered, had she been railroaded into this? She glanced toward JT, noticing how the night-dark shirt made his silvery eyes even more dramatic in contrast. Oh, yeah. Now she remembered how she'd wound up here. She'd been too dazed to put up a sustained, coherent argument.

Also, everyone had ganged up on her. After the way Leslie had doted on JT the other day, Kenzie wasn't surprised by her daughter's behavior. She was more suspicious of Sean's motivation, though, and Ann's quick agreement. Surely her always responsible sister wasn't planning to do anything stupid?

Since they were a bit ahead of the dinner crowd and it was the middle of the week, they were seated quickly in a section of the restaurant designated Magical Dining. Waitresses wore witches' hats, and framed posters on the walls were from family-friendly movies ranging from *Bedknobs and Broomsticks* to *The Wizard of Oz* to more recent films. The spacious center of the building was devoted to the nine-hole golf course one had to pass to get a table; various dining rooms branched off like spokes from the main area. Drew forgot about his stomach long enough to scope out which holes looked the most challenging. Leslie was grinning as if she'd walked into one of her favorite books.

"So how'd you know about this place?" Kenzie asked.

"I'm an uncle." Sean helped Ann get the high chair situated. "I've become something of a regular here. I can highly recommend the wizard's filet."

Everyone took a chair, and somehow Kenzie found herself seated beside JT, which she'd hoped to avoid. Still, an undisciplined part of her—the old impulsive Kenzie—thrilled at his nearness and the subtly male scent of his soap. His eyes met hers, and she felt as if they were in their own little bubble, since the kids were busily pointing out decorations to each other and Sean and Ann were both admiring a cooing Abigail.

"Tell me about this new painting," Kenzie invited.

"It's not really a *new* work. Sean found a couple that had seen one of my bigger pieces and wanted to own a smaller re-creation."

"That still takes talent." She recalled his mural at the museum. "Which you definitely have."

He ducked his head in modest acknowledgment, the gesture endearingly boyish. "Thank you. I did manage to update the piece slightly. I'm happy with how it turned out."

"I can tell. You look…different. Good."

"You, on the other hand, always look good." He flashed a brief but charged smile of masculine appreciation.

Warmth blossomed inside her, as if she'd just taken her first rich sip of hot cocoa and could feel the chocolate melting through her body. After a moment, she realized the table had grown quiet. No one else seemed to be conversing anymore. They were, she realized, watching *her* watch JT. Leslie seemed delighted enough to dance a jig, Drew was scowling and Ann actually winked at her.

Kenzie cleared her throat, glancing desperately toward Sean. "So, the wizard's filet is good then?"

LEANING BACK IN HER CHAIR, feeling pleasantly stuffed, Kenzie smiled at Sean. "I have to hand it to you, you're great at picking out restaurants."

"I'm great at everything," he declared.

Over the past hour, Kenzie had grown accustomed to the man's joyfully outrageous nature. Sean was a flirt, but not in a sensual or discriminating way. He was the kind of man who could charm any woman between two and two hundred. He was fun to be around, yet so unlike JT that it was difficult to imagine how the men had become friends. Was it a case of opposite personalities bonding because their differences complemented each other, or had JT once been more like his business partner?

When Sean took the kids to get golf supplies and Ann excused herself to check Abby's diaper in the restroom, Kenzie found herself alone with JT and her curiosity. "Sean takes some getting used to," she observed with a smile.

"Let me know how long it takes. I still haven't managed it," he teased.

"You've known him a long time?"

He nodded, staring into the remains of his iced tea. "More than a lifetime, it feels like. He does catch me off guard sometimes. Accepting the commission for the Owenbys' painting, for instance. Personality-wise, we don't have much in common, but he looks out for me."

"Ann and I are kind of the reverse," she said. "As kids, we had little in common and were perfectly happy to go our separate ways. But I've enjoyed reconnecting with her now that we're older and have more life experience to help us relate. I don't have much practice doing it, but I want to look out for her. Sean wouldn't hit on a married woman, would he?"

JT laughed. "Is that why you think he went along with Leslie's idea to eat together? Actually, I think it's *you* he noticed."

"What?"

"The first time he ever saw you, he walked into my apartment and called you 'hot.'" JT frowned. "I didn't much like that."

"Hot?" she echoed in disbelief. "Are you sure he wasn't talking about someone else?"

"Have you looked in the mirror lately? Those eyes alone. If I could paint..." He shifted in his chair. "I don't mean to make you uncomfortable."

She wasn't discomfited. On the contrary, she was becoming aroused. She swallowed, idly wondering if he ever painted nudes. Wondering if, after waddling through pregnancy with twins and now approaching thirty, she'd be entirely at ease letting a man see her body. She wasn't eighteen anymore, but the way JT was looking at her, he didn't appear to be cataloging the faint laugh lines at the corners of her eyes or the few-but-stubborn gray hairs that had recently appeared near her part.

"So, are you two ready to go for it?" a voice asked.

Kenzie whipped her head around to see Sean's smirk.

"Golf?" he reminded them, extending a pink-tipped club in her direction. "To the links!"

Ann declined play in favor of sitting on a bench while she gave Abigail the bottle she'd brought. "You five go ahead and have fun."

"It won't be mere fun," Sean said with mock gravity. "It will be a slaughter. I'm the Tiger Woods of the miniature-golf circuit."

"Oh, yeah?" Drew challenged. "I'll bet I get a hole in one before you!"

Sean grinned. "We'll see about that, youngster. I was swinging a nine iron before you were born."

"That's because you're *old,*" Drew said, his expression one of faux sympathy.

Laughing out loud, Sean made a smart-aleck retort that Kenzie didn't hear.

"He is good with kids," she remarked to JT as Leslie set her ball on the tee.

JT's face contorted for a second. "Yeah, he is."

"What?" she asked. It wasn't the first time she'd seen his expression darken at the mention of children, but now she found she couldn't leave well enough alone. Despite herself, she wanted to understand, and soothe the shadows from his eyes.

He took a deep breath. "Holly and I were expecting. That was my wife's name—Holly. We'd asked Sean to be the godfather."

Oh, God. Kenzie couldn't begin to comprehend the depth of his loss. As with the other day, it was on the tip of her tongue to say she was sorry, but the words were so painfully inadequate. Instead, unthinkingly, she reached out and squeezed his hand.

He glanced up, astonishment on his face, then down at their joined fingers. He returned her grip, his strong and warm. Awareness pulsed between them. If such simple, platonic contact could send sensation thrumming through her, what would it be like if he really *touched* her?

In recent memory, people had reached out to her as a mother, sister or daughter. The kids weren't so old that they were above cuddling when there was a storm raging outside, or one of them was sick. Ann hugged her, their mother stroked her hair whenever Kenzie managed to come home.

It had been forever since she'd been touched as a woman.

"I…" JT's voice was thick, a husky caress. "I think it's your turn."

Glancing at the putting green, Kenzie found the others were indeed waiting. "Right. My turn." She set down the sky-blue ball and hit it with more oomph than strictly necessary. It struck a woman at the third tee in the back of the calf.

Ouch. "Sorry!" Kenzie called, cringing.

Her children snickered, and Sean halfheartedly chided them while trying to stifle his own laugh. Even JT had sparks of amusement illuminating his eyes.

"I'm a little out of practice at this," she told him breathlessly.

He caught her chin between his fingers for a fraction of a moment before letting go. "That's okay. So am I."

ANN TACTFULLY WAITED until the twins had gone to bed before broaching the subject of the evening's activities. "They certainly seemed to have fun tonight."

"Yeah. It was a good place to take them."

"And did *you* enjoy yourself?"

"Uh-huh. Are you all done in the bathroom? I was planning to hop in the shower."

Her sister leaned against the arm of the couch. "Would that be a cold shower?"

"I hope not. If the hot water heater's on the fritz, we should let Mr. C. know," Kenzie babbled. "He's really quite handy. You hear horror stories about apartment supers in the city, but—"

"Mackenzie."

"Don't ask about JT."

"If you tell me, I won't have to ask."

Kenzie groaned, torn between the need to discuss him with someone and the fear that vocalizing her budding feelings would make them even more real. She was here only six more weeks, then she was moving to her Perfect House and he, hopefully, would continue rediscovering his former joy of painting. She did not need extra complications in her life, and it would be a lot easier to avoid temptation when she wasn't bumping into tall, dark and complicated every time she opened her apartment door.

"He's attractive," she allowed, feeling as foolish as if she'd just proclaimed the Sahara "a bit sandy."

"Tell me something I don't know."

"He lost a wife and unborn baby."

Ann's breath hitched. "That's awful."

"Yeah." Kenzie stared into space. "The first few times I saw him, he never even smiled. Understandable, I'd say."

"He was smiling plenty tonight. Whenever he looked at you, for instance."

Kenzie tried to shrug off the observation. "I think he was just in a good mood. He's expressed frustration over not being able to paint. I guess he was creatively blocked. But now he's finished a piece he can be proud of. I noticed as soon as he stepped out of his apartment that he looked happy."

"He looked happy to see *you*."

"Ann, honestly, you might be overromanticizing the situation."

Her sister snorted. "Have you ever known me to romanticize anything? At all?"

"For all I know, he's still in love with his wife. Besides, he's all wrong for me."

"Which part of attractive, successful men who are good-natured about spending time with your kids turns you off?"

"You don't know him well enough to call him successful."

"Didn't you say he was specially invited to paint a mural for one of the city's museums?"

"And just because he was good-natured at dinner… Artistic types are notoriously moody. He was happy tonight, but what about the next time he gets stuck? The twins have already had one man in their lives whose emotional temperament was unreliable, who followed his muse at the expense of his family. I wasn't kidding when I talked about JT not smiling the first few times I saw him. I know he's capable of darker spells and, given his loss, I certainly empathize. But I won't put the kids through that again."

The teasing light had gone out of Ann's eyes. "The kids or you? I remember when you worshipped Mick, dreamed of all the places you'd see together and the family you'd build."

"Which was stupid. What did I think we were going to do, backpack two babies on tour?"

"You were eighteen and thought that anything was possible with love." Ann shrugged. "That's not a crime. I can't imagine how disillusioned you must have been to divorce him. That took courage, to do what was right for you and the kids."

In some ways, Ann was right. It did take a bitter kind of courage to admit you'd been so wrong about someone for so long.

"I just hope," she continued softly, "that you also have the guts to try again when the time comes."

Panic over how potent her feelings for JT were becoming made Kenzie defensive. "I don't think you can lecture me about courage. Why aren't you at home, bravely trying to work things out with your husband instead of being here, once again giving me advice on how I should live my life?"

Ann's face went slack.

"Oh. Oh, Ann, forget I said that. That was just plain bitchy."

"No argument there," she said with a feeble smile. "But there was some truth in it."

"A teeny, tiny kernel. I didn't mean to snap at you like that. I'm a horrible sister. I even called Forrest," she blurted in a fit of self-recrimination.

"What? When?"

"A couple of nights ago. I thought he needed a kick in the pants, figuratively speaking."

"His pants must be very well padded. Don't you think if he cared about me at all he would have done, I don't know, *something?*"

This was a tricky area. "You know him better than I do. As you pointed out, even though he's older, you took the lead in the relationship. Maybe he wants to make things better but isn't sure exactly how. Maybe he thinks that, since you left, time and space are what you want and he's trying to give you that."

Ann said nothing.

"Please forget I made that comment," Kenzie pleaded. "You know you're welcome here as long as you like."

Ann nodded, but seemed subdued. By morning, however, she was smiling and joking with the kids about their putt-putt efforts the previous night. The school year was under way, and her family seemed comparatively happy. Kenzie went to work ensconced in a false sense of security. Then came Friday afternoon and the phone call at work she'd been subconsciously dreading.

"Kenzie Green speaking."

"Hi, this is Teena Arnold, the vice principal over at Carter. I'm calling about your son, Drew." The woman's tone was pleasant enough, but that didn't stop Kenzie from gripping the receiver tighter.

It's only the third day! What's he done? "Is there a problem, Ms. Arnold?"

"Not exactly, but we were wondering if it would be possible for you to come in this afternoon. Maybe you, myself, Drew and his teacher could have a little chat."

"About? I mean, of course I'll be there. I was just wondering…"

"Oh, I don't think it's a major worry, but Mrs. Frazer has some concerns about Drew's attitude, and some observations she'd like to share with you."

That sounded innocuous enough. Kenzie exhaled in relief that he hadn't started a fight by being overly competitive in P.E., hadn't stopped up all the toilets in the boys' bathroom, or done other destructive things she didn't even want to imagine.

Just some "observations." How bad could that be?

It was school policy that siblings not be in the same class, and Kenzie had met both the kids' teachers before the first day. When she walked into the vice principal's office Friday afternoon, she couldn't help again thinking that Mrs. Frazer, taller with stern, patrician features, was like Abbott to Mrs. Kane's Costello. Leslie's teacher was short, round, jolly, with a higher pitched voice that squeaked slightly when she spoke on a topic that excited her.

Drew was slouched in a chair, looking miserable, and Mrs. Frazer stood behind him. The vice principal, a silver-haired woman in pearls, leaned across her desk to shake Kenzie's hand.

"I'm so glad you were able to make time for us, Mrs. Green," the older woman said warmly.

"My kids are my priority." Kenzie tried to catch Drew's eye, wanting him to know she was on his side. "Honey, do you want to tell me what's going on?"

He shrugged. "Some stupid paper. I did the assignment. I didn't do anything wrong!"

Mrs. Frazer clucked her tongue. "Calling it a 'stupid' paper isn't productive dialogue, Andrew."

Kenzie resisted the urge to roll her eyes. Productive dialogue? Lofty expectations, indeed, especially since boys his age often considered armpit farts a valid form of communication. "What was the assignment, Drew?"

"Supposed to write about family," he mumbled.

She groaned inwardly. Was this about his dad? Both Mrs. Kane and Mrs. Frazer knew the kids came from a divorced home, but Kenzie hadn't expected it to be an issue so soon. After the twins had survived Father's Day with no word from their actual father, she'd hoped the next big hurdle wouldn't be until Christmas. Would it be wrong to buy gifts and say they were from Mick?

"Drew, you're not in any trouble," the vice principal interjected. "We just all care about you very much—"

He scoffed. "You don't even know me."

Kenzie squeezed his shoulder warningly, but the grandmotherly woman seemed unperturbed.

"We wanted to talk a little about your feelings and make your mother aware of them. Would you like to read her your essay?"

"Not really."

Mrs. Frazer had produced a pair of reading glasses and a piece of lined notebook paper. "If I may, Mrs. Green, here's a section of what your son wrote. 'My friend Jimmy back home has a cool family. He plays football every Saturday with his dad and brothers in the yard. I don't have brothers or a dad or a yard. I live in a small apartment with my mom, sister, crazy aunt and her stinky baby.'"

"Drew." Kenzie wanted to say a half-dozen things at once and landed on, "Aunt Ann is certainly not crazy."

"She cries as much as Abby, if she doesn't think anyone's looking."

"Women who've recently had babies can be a little emotional, honey."

"*I* didn't ask her to have a baby! Or to move in with us. We're too crowded already, and she and Uncle Forrest have a huge house. Can I go live with him? Just us guys."

She couldn't really see Forrest tossing around the pigskin with a little boy; the professor was more likely to consider checking the morning stocks together a bonding activity.

The vice principal leaned forward. "We certainly aren't advocating that he go live with anyone else, but it does seem as if he's surrounded by a lot of female influence. He's welcome to speak to our guidance counselor anytime he chooses—she's a wonderful listener and the kids all seem to respond to her—but Mrs. Frazer and I thought that perhaps he could benefit from a male presence in his life. A mentor of sorts. If his father's not available to help—"

"Not at this time," Kenzie said flatly.

"Then perhaps this Uncle Forrest?"

"Ah…that's a possibility." A complicated, awkward possibility, but worth discussing with Ann if it was in Drew's best interest.

"What about JT?" Drew said suddenly.

Kenzie's jaw dropped. "JT?"

"Yeah, he could be my mental."

"Oh, I don't think so, honey. I wasn't even sure you liked him. And he's so busy with his painting…."

"Yeah." Drew's chin thrust out. "Everyone's always so busy." Her heart hurt.

The vice principal cleared her throat. "Well, we've certainly given you a lot to think about over the three-day holiday, haven't we, Mrs. Green? You and Drew talk, and let us know if we can be of any help."

"Thanks." Kenzie walked with Drew to the door and wished both of the other women a good Labor Day weekend.

Kenzie had arranged for Leslie to ride home solo on the bus and for Ann to meet her at the stop. That gave Kenzie and her son a few minutes to talk privately in the car. If he didn't want to, should she push? It turned out that worry was for nothing. He started firing questions at her even before he had his seat belt buckled.

"Is Aunt Ann living with us because Uncle Forrest doesn't love her anymore? Will Abigail grow up without a daddy, too? Is she going to move with us into the new house?"

"No, honey. You know how sometimes I have to separate you and Leslie when you're fighting?"

Despite his sullen attitude, he flashed a mischievous grin. "You mean when we're annoying you?"

"Ann and Forrest didn't want to fight, so they're kind of giving each other a time-out. I don't know how much longer she'll be staying with us, but she is not moving into the new house."

"Are you sure?"

Not entirely. "Why did you suggest JT as a mentor?" She would have been less surprised to hear him mention Sean. Though he didn't technically know the blond man well, they'd certainly hit it off. With JT, Drew was pricklier than a den full of hedgehogs.

"Dunno," the boy muttered. "He's a guy. He lives even closer than Uncle Forrest."

And JT had officially been on more outings with Drew than his biological father had all year. "Those are logical reasons," she agreed. "But I thought you didn't like him."

"I don't like art. At least, I didn't think so. Some of the stuff at that museum was kinda cool, I guess. Besides, Leslie's a suck-up. If you and JT start dating, I want to make sure he likes me, too. Or she'll get better presents at Christmas."

"Drew!" Kenzie gripped the steering wheel tightly, trying not to veer into oncoming traffic. *Back way the hell up, son.* "I already told you I didn't have any plans to date JT. I hardly think you need to start worrying about Christmas presents."

"Did you ever plan for you and Dad to, you know, end up living apart? Do you think he planned to be a better dad?"

How had her nine-year-old become so wise in the ways of the world? "I know it bothers your daddy that he isn't doing a better job. He's said so on more than one occasion."

"Then why doesn't he try harder?" Drew demanded.

"Sometimes it's hard for people to change, even when they really, really want to."

"If he ever gets a hit song on the radio, I'm not listening to it!"

"If you think that will make you feel better."

He stared out the window, not speaking again until she pulled into a parking space. "Mom, do you think JT would teach me how to paint?"

"I, uh… Honey, I really don't know. He's been having a hard time with painting lately, and we won't be here much longer," she reminded him. But Drew looked so unexpectedly crestfallen that she heard herself say, "I'll ask him. No promises, though!"

Life would be so much easier, she reflected, without promises. Fewer broken vows to spouses and disappointments to children. Even privately, promises could trip up a person. She'd sworn to be independent and responsible, avoiding men who might hurt her or have the power to wound her kids, yet she'd begun thinking of JT at random moments and as she fell asleep at night. Now her reticent son was beginning to carve out a place in his life and affections for the artist.

Please, please don't hurt us. Even if it were a promise she had the right to ask for, was it one he'd be able to keep?

Chapter Ten

As soon as Kenzie walked into the apartment, she saw a huge floral arrangement dominating the coffee table. No point in asking who they were for, considering Ann's giddy expression.

"Can you believe he sent flowers?" she asked, beaming in Kenzie and Drew's direction. Then she sobered. "Everything go okay at the school?"

"Fine," Kenzie replied, cutting her eyes toward Drew and hoping to convey to her sister that they'd talk later. "Leslie make it home all right?"

Ann nodded. "She's in her room listening to her iPod and doing homework."

"What a nerd," Drew said. "We have three whole days before class."

"Yes, but your sister knows better than to procrastinate," Kenzie said pointedly.

"I guess I should go work."

She tousled his hair. "Good guess."

As he shuffled down the hall, she bent to inhale the fragrance of the purple and yellow bouquet. The last time a man had sent *her* flowers had been her boss in Raindrop when she'd discovered an accounting error in the bank's favor.

"So, was there a card?" she asked her sister.

"It said 'I miss you. Forrest.' If it hadn't had his name on it, I might have thought JT sent these for you."

Kenzie tried not to imagine how she'd feel if he made such a gesture. "'I miss you'? Simple, classic, to the point. I like it. Did you call to let him know you got them?"

"I left a message." Ann floated to the kitchen, where she lifted a pot lid and stirred something that smelled divine. "I told him thank-you. And that I miss him, too. And that Abby misses the way he sings to her when she's fussy."

"Forrest sings?" Kenzie couldn't quite picture that.

"Yeah, he has a surprisingly good voice. I try to soothe her with lullabies, but it's not the same." Ann worried her bottom lip with her teeth. "Do you think it's selfish of me, being here and separating her from her dad at a formative age?"

"I don't think you've scarred her for life, no, but I'm sure she'd be happy to go home. Drew asked me today if…"

"If what?"

"Well, if you were planning to move into the new house with us."

Ann gave a horrified bark of laughter, then clapped her hand over her mouth. "Oh, dear. Has my being here upset him?"

"He loves you. He really loves your cooking. He may not fully appreciate Abby yet, but that will come as they both get older. His teacher, however, is worried about estrogen overload. He's living with a sister, mom, aunt and tiny female cousin with a wardrobe of pink. They think he could benefit from some male influence. I wondered the same thing last spring, when he kept angling to get extra attention and playing time from his coaches."

Ann poured two glasses of ice water, handing one to Kenzie. "Are you thinking about calling Mick?"

Sipping the water, Kenzie considered the possible outcomes of such a call. "He's notoriously difficult to get ahold of. He doesn't stay in one place long, his cell phone gets turned off whenever he's low on funds, and he's slow to return messages. That said, if I *could* reach him and I told him about the vice principal's concerns, he'd ask if there was anything he could do and would immediately want to talk to Drew. He'd promise to come spend a weekend of special father-son time—he might even do it, if a gig didn't crop up in the meantime—but if he came and spent a wonderful weekend with Drew, it would hurt Les. And if he came and spent a wonderful weekend with both of them, full of resolutions to be a better dad and see them more, it would just leave more pieces for me to pick up when another six months pass before we hear from him again."

"That sounds like a no on calling him, then."

"He means well." Kenzie set her glass on the counter. "But intentions aren't enough. There needs to be action, follow-through." Speaking of well-intentioned promises… "I told Drew I'd ask JT for a favor this weekend. I expect to see him at the tenants Labor Day picnic. Think we could whip up some really great dessert I could use as a bribe?"

Ann struck a goofy femme fatale pose. "You sure you don't want to bargain with sexual favors, instead?"

"Rhiannon!" Kenzie paused, her mind departing on naughty flights of fancy. "We'll call that Plan B."

As JT STARED AT HIS reflection in the bedroom mirror, he was struck simultaneously by two absurd bits of behavior—he was whistling a jaunty tune *and* he was considering changing clothes, inexplicably second-guessing whether his denim shorts and faded Shakespeare Tavern T-shirt were too informal for the annual rooftop picnic. The ringing phone interrupted his contemplation and he answered, half his mind still on wardrobe issues.

"Yo," Sean said in greeting. "Just wanted to let you know the Owenbys were thrilled. I knew they would be, but I thought you'd want to hear they loved the painting."

"Thanks," JT said absently, carrying the cordless phone toward the closet. Well, no wonder he'd gone with this shirt, he realized a second later. It was one of the few that had been clean and on a hanger. "Have you ever known me to be jaunty?"

"Not on purpose. There was that one Christmas party, though, with the eggnog incident."

"You've conveniently confused me with you."

"So I have. What's up? Feeling jaunty?"

JT had no idea what he was feeling. It was as if after months of living in the relative safety of dark numbness, he'd emerged into a kaleidoscope of bright emotion. Not an entirely pleasant sensation. As with a numb limb that had been "awakened," there were sharp needles of pain.

Along with returning responsibilities, he thought, glancing around as if seeing the dim room for the first time. He was an artist, for crying out loud, and there wasn't a damn thing hanging on the walls in here. When was the last time he'd made the bed? The pile of dirty clothes against the wall probably qualified for historic landmark status.

JT frowned. "I gotta go, man."

"Tell Kenzie I said hello."

"I didn't say anything about seeing her."

"You were behaving even more bizarrely than normal, so I intuited you must be nervous about spending time with a certain cute blonde. Plus, when we were at dinner, I overheard mention of the Labor Day picnic. Tell Mrs. Sanchez I said hi, too. Her cooking has ruined me for all other women."

"Why should I be nervous about seeing Kenzie? She's my neighbor. I see her all the time. She's…nice."

"I'll say."

"Don't think about her in that tone of voice." A wave of irrational possessiveness rose inside him.

"No lewd disrespect intended. I admire her wit and parenting skills and how adorably protective she is of her sister. But none of that precludes noticing just how—"

"I'm serious."

"All right." Sean paused. "So why *are* you nervous about seeing her?"

"Because I want to," he said finally. It had been a long time since he'd let himself look forward to something, since he'd truly wanted *anything*. Even though he'd complained about not being able to paint, that had been more frustration than the desire to create. On a basic level, he wanted Kenzie.

He wasn't sure if it would ever deepen into a more complicated emotion or if he was too damaged for that. For the time being, just wanting to be near her was something to savor. A rare gift he'd doubted he would experience again.

Now that he'd managed to answer Sean's question, though, JT was plagued with one of his own—did Kenzie want him?

IN HER MIND, Kenzie always associated September and the start of each new school year with the changing seasons and the crisp bite of fall. In reality, however, today was approaching record-breaking highs and the baking heat stole her breath as she stepped onto the roof. Three minutes up here and she'd be sweating like a petty criminal during a tax audit.

A chorus of friendly hellos met her, and she smiled at Mrs.

Sanchez and Mr. C. Alicia from downstairs approached and offered to carry the glass dish over to the food table. But Kenzie didn't see—

"Excuse me." JT's voice was an apologetic rumble and she felt more than saw him draw up short to avoid colliding with her.

She turned to look over her shoulder, drinking him in with her eyes. "No, it's my fault. I shouldn't be blocking the doorway." With him so close, taking a step away was the last thing she wanted to do, but she suspected he'd like to set down the heavy cooler he was toting.

"I don't cook," he said sheepishly. "Ice and sodas are my traditional contribution."

"Hey, don't knock the ice and soda. On a scorcher like today, they'll be a hit."

"Maybe next year we can do this in the parking garage instead. Think of all that shade. Then again, the view's nicer here."

Got that right, she thought, unable to resist watching as he walked past her toward the folding tables.

A moment later, he returned, carrying two different kinds of soft drink. "Take your pick," he offered.

"Thank you." She unscrewed the lid of one, toying with the plastic.

"Where's everyone else?" he asked.

"They'll be up soon. Leslie's helping get the baby ready, and Drew had to finish his video game level before he saved his progress." All true, but Kenzie had ducked out ahead of her family on purpose, crossing her fingers for a chance to speak with JT alone. "I was hoping to run into you this afternoon."

"Oh?" His eyes were a hot liquid silver, and she almost blushed under their scrutiny.

She nodded, leaning against a section of decorative railing. "I need to talk to you about something. If you have a minute?"

"Fire at will."

The phrase might be more apt than he'd intended. He seemed a fairly private man, and she'd wondered if he ever felt under attack from his temporary but invasive neighbors. Leslie pushed for his company every time she saw him; Drew was barely civil. Now there were Ann and the baby, too. While JT had never complained, Kenzie suspected he could sometimes hear Abigail crying. Knowing he'd been expecting a child of his own, she better understood the way he quickly glanced away from the infant when he encountered her.

She swallowed. "My son, Drew? I realize you don't know us very well, but I'm sure you've noticed he's…working through some issues."

JT laid his arm across the rail, not touching her but close enough that she could feel the warmth from his skin. "Artists are supposed to be observant. I may not have known you long, but I think I'm starting to know you well. The twins are angry, with good reason, but they're amazing kids with lots of talent and strength. And you're a great mom who's doing a hell of a job with little help."

At twenty-eight, having someone praise her ability as a mother was about the headiest compliment she could imagine, far more potent than if he'd told her she had a lovely smile or shapely legs. "Thank you, but you give me too much credit. Ann's been helping, too."

"Seems to me that's a two-way street. Is she here to assist you, or are you giving her sanctuary through a tough time?"

"Both, I guess. Although her presence is part of why I need to talk to you."

His eyebrows winged skyward.

"Drew's teacher and vice principal called me in for a short conference yesterday. Apparently, one of the things he's unhappy about is being constantly surrounded by females."

JT grinned into his drink. "He'll grow out of that. In a few years, girls won't seem so bad."

"Even then, I suspect his mom, aunt and sister won't rate very high on his cool list. Meanwhile, the staff at his school feel he'd benefit from more, um, male influence in his life. A role model or teacher."

"I suppose that makes sense," JT said carefully, obviously starting to question how this applied to him.

"And then Drew surprised me on the way home from school with a request." She took a deep breath. "It was more a request for you, really. He wanted to know if you could show him a couple of things about painting."

"You want me to teach your son to paint?"

"I... It was Drew's idea, but it fits in nicely with the teacher's suggestion that he occasionally hang out with a guy." For the next five weeks, anyway. "They don't have to be formal, scheduled lessons. Unless that's what you want! I could even pay you whatever the comparable rate—" She stopped abruptly when she realized she had no idea what private art lessons with an acclaimed painter might cost. Wasn't she supposed to be saving up for all the miscellaneous expenses that came with a move?

"I don't want your money, Kenzie." With the metallic glint of panic in his eyes, he didn't look as if he wanted anything to do with her. Did he even realize he'd taken a step back?

"Never mind. This wasn't very well thought out," she admitted. "It's just that I promised Drew I'd ask, and now I have. So—"

"I'll do it."

"What?"

He scraped a hand over his jaw, gazing at something unseen beyond her. "Not to bash your ex, but I know what it's like to be hurt by your own dad. I can't make that better for Drew. I don't want to be a father or anyone's substitute father figure, but maybe I can be a friend. At the very least, I can let him come over to my apartment and throw some paint at a canvas on a semi-regular basis.

"Of course, if your son turns out to be some kind of prodigy, I want partial credit for having discovered him."

The joke he tacked on to lighten the moment barely penetrated her wonder that he'd agreed to help, when it clearly wouldn't have been his first choice. Fierce gratitude crashed through her. Rising on tiptoes, she swayed toward him. He didn't seem the huggy type, but perhaps he'd permit a quick peck of thanks on the cheek? He could easily evade her if he didn't want her this close.

It was hard to say which one of them redirected her intended gesture. Had she been deceiving herself in that split second when she'd told herself she was aiming for his cheek, or was it JT who'd had something else in mind when he bent his head down? Maybe it was both of them.

Regardless of how or why, JT's mouth, superficially cool from the icy soda, but burning hot beyond that, was pressed to hers.

Her lips parted in a sigh, and he explored them gently, running his tongue over the seam, sucking her bottom lip— a slight but intimate tug that made her tremble. She felt an answering pull deep inside her, and opened her mouth even farther. Cupping the back of her head in one large hand, he accepted the silent invitation. At the first velvety stroke of his tongue against hers, sensation shot through her. She clasped his shirtfront, making an involuntary sound that was only a few decibels shy of an honest-to-goodness moan. The man could seriously kiss.

Oh, dear. She was *kissing* JT! In full view of the other tenants, including the fifteen-year-old who sometimes babysat for Kenzie's kids. Kids who could show up on this very roof at any second and catch their mom making out like Alicia's boy-crazy, teenage sister. It was that thought that overrode every other physical impulse she was experiencing and allowed her to pull free of his embrace.

"I j-just wanted to say thank-you," she stammered, feeling like an idiot.

Two small lines of confusion puckered his brow. "For the kiss?"

"No, before. That's what I was doing. Trying to thank you."

He looked startled for a moment, then threw his head back and laughed. "Remind me to do you lots of favors."

The suggestive pleasure in his tone kept her from feeling she was being mocked, and she smiled back. His uncharacteristic show of humor made her even more self-conscious, though, and she glanced around nervously to see if they had an audience. The Wilders from the first floor were sniping at each other as usual and seemed oblivious to everyone else. Alicia was standing at the food table, rolling her eyes at the way her older sister flirted with the building's resident college student. Mrs. Sanchez and her oldest daughter were furtively whispering to each other, and Kenzie experienced a frisson of unease, hoping that their hushed conversation was family gossip.

"Do you think anyone noticed?" she asked JT. "That was really irresponsible of me."

He brushed her hair away from her face. "It was just a kiss."

"Just?"

"Poor word choice. In all honesty, I'm not sure what words to use." He took a sip of his drink, glancing away before he spoke again. She appreciated the chance to regain her composure. "I plan to be up here for a while, if Drew wants to talk to me about coming over to paint."

"Thank you."

"You're welcome. Though I'm partial to the way you said it last time."

Unconsciously, she rubbed the pad of her thumb over her bottom lip. "So am I, but I didn't mean for it to be a spectator event." She'd all but sworn to her son that she wouldn't date JT. How betrayed would the kid feel if he'd seen her unguarded moment of lust? As habitually angry as he already was, she couldn't imagine what it would do to him if he felt he couldn't count on her.

"Next time," JT said softly, "we'll have to make sure it's just the two of us."

Her pulse raced. Did she want there to be a next time? Ludicrous question. Of course she wanted it. She ached with wanting. But did that mean kissing him again, letting him kiss her, was wise?

Noting her silence, he amended, "If there's a next time."

"Right."

If. A small, seemingly insignificant word for such a dizzying wealth of possibilities.

Chapter Eleven

Kenzie tossed and turned in bed, trying not to notice how large the mattress seemed tonight. There was way more space than one woman needed all by herself—even a woman as restless as her. She sat, irritably kicking at the sheets tangled among her calves. The apartment was unbearably hot. *I'll call Mr. C. in the morning, get him to double-check that the air conditioner's working properly.*

Her sigh echoed in the dark stillness of the room. Was she really deluded enough to convince herself that the problem was the AC and not that kiss she and JT had shared this afternoon? Maybe the reason she couldn't sleep was because she knew he was right across the hall. Was he painting during these late hours? Snoozing peacefully in his own bed? Or was he, like her, reliving the heady taste of their kiss, the contrast between the heat of their bodies pressed together and the slight, merciful breeze that had rippled over them for a moment?

She closed her eyes, remembering that moment, the sensations that had melted through her at the first touch of his mouth. *Bad idea.* Images like that were not going to soothe her into a more restful state.

Kicking her feet over the side of the bed, she thought of

all the times she'd heard people recommend a glass of milk to fight insomnia. What about a giant bowl of ice cream? There should be plenty of milk in that, right?

Barefoot, she padded down the hallway, slowing when she heard a voice. At first she thought it might be Leslie talking in her sleep, but then realized it was Ann in the living room. She must be up with Abigail. Kenzie crept forward in a silent tiptoe, so as not to disturb the baby if Ann almost had her asleep.

"You know I do," her sister was saying softly, "but that's just the point…I don't *want* to come home so everything can be just like it was. If I'd been happy with everything as is, I wouldn't have left."

Kenzie froze. Her sister wasn't talking to the baby; she was on the phone with Forrest.

Suddenly there came the sound of a sultry, un-Ann-like chuckle. "Okay, that can stay the same. Wait—Kenzie's got another call, so… How should I know who's calling her at this hour? Of *course* I'm not inventing a reason to get out of our conversation, you lunatic." Despite her words, her voice was tender.

Someone was calling this late? Kenzie coughed delicately, alerting Ann to her presence as she rounded the corner.

"Hello?" Ann was pulling herself into a sitting position on the sofa, her eyes wide in the dim lamplight. "Yes, actually, here she is now."

"Who is it?" Kenzie asked, her mind irrationally leaping to JT. Not much of a leap, really, since her thoughts had been on him all evening. In addition to being a devastating kisser, he'd been remarkably friendly and patient with her son when Drew had finally shown up to scarf down three plate-fuls of food.

Ann cupped her hand over the cordless receiver. "It's Mick. Were you expecting his call?"

"Mick?" Shock paralyzed her as she reached for the phone. "The Mick I married?"

Ann nodded, making no attempt to hide her curiosity. "You think everything's all right?" she whispered.

"Only one way to find out." Kenzie took a deep breath. As she held the phone to her ear, she heard throbbing bass and background chatter. He was probably calling from a club somewhere. "Hello?"

"Mackenzie." He greeted her with gruff affection. "It's good to hear your voice."

Several sarcastic retorts came to mind about how he could hear it more often, but she bit her tongue as she carried the phone to her bedroom. Mick was who he was. Though she could harangue an apology out of him, that wouldn't make him less likely to lose track of time if he was jamming with the band, or more likely to pay his cellular service bill.

"I got your message that you were moving to Atlanta."

"That was weeks ago," she pointed out gently. "Thank goodness I wasn't trying to get ahold of you because of an emergency."

He gave a self-deprecating chuckle. "Hell, what right-thinking person would call *me* in an emergency? We both know I stink in a crisis. The kids are lucky to have you as a mother, Mac. You're better at everything than I am. Except maybe an inverted guitar chord."

"It's true the kids won't inherit any musical ability from me."

There was a pause, followed by rustling and the fading of ambient noise. He'd either gone outside or walked somewhere more private. When he spoke again, it was easy to hear the waver of emotion in his voice. "How are they?"

"If you'd called a couple of hours ago, you could have asked them that yourself." With a sigh, she got back in bed. "They miss you."

"I miss them, too. Which is part of the reason I've quit."

"Quit what?"

"Performing. I've left the band."

She couldn't have been more astounded if he said he was giving up *breathing*. "You're kidding."

"You know I don't kid about music."

That was true. "Are you looking for another band? Or attempting a solo career?"

"No, I'm serious. I've quit. You reach an age when you can't keep lying to yourself. If it was gonna happen for me… 'Course, the industry's in my blood now. I've met dozens of musicians in the past few years, many of them really talented. Maybe I can help."

"I don't understand."

"I'm going to represent other musicians! I've made connections," he said proudly. "Just because I wasn't able to make them work for me the way I'd hoped doesn't mean those connections won't come through for the right band, the right singer with that 'it' factor."

"Um…" She wanted to be supportive, but she'd always seen him as more adept at making music than having business sense. Even if he were successful in this new venture, would he be happy watching someone else reap the accolades he'd dreamed of for more than a decade?

"In fact, I'm out tonight with new clients! I'm going to focus on their set and help them figure out how to improve it before next Tuesday. They've got a gig in Nashville that could be their big break!"

God. She prayed for patience as she battled back the unwanted déjà vu. If she had a dollar for every "gig" that was supposed to have built a career, she could single-handedly buy one of the houses in Ann's neighborhood.

"I've saved the best news for last!" Mick told her excitedly.

Her body tensed in nervous anticipation of what other bombshells were in store.

"Atlanta's developing quite the recording scene. If all goes well, I'll be in the city on a semi-regular basis. The kids and I can reconnect."

"That would be... Mick, you're free to come see them anytime. You don't have to wait for a professional reason to come to the city." It would have been great if he'd make plans surrounding, for instance, the kids' birthday. Or the upcoming winter holidays. Thanksgiving would be here before she knew it, Christmas close on its heels.

"Don't worry, it'll be soon! But I should get back inside before the boys get started. The opening number is really important for winning over the audience, setting the right mood. Hey, don't tell the kids yet about my coming to see them? It would be a cool surprise."

She wasn't sure. Drew in particular might need some time to sort out how he felt about seeing his dad, but she agreed not to tell them just yet. After all, Mick's definition of "soon" wasn't necessarily the same one the rest of the English-speaking world used. The less she told the twins now, the less disappointed they might be when his plans unraveled later.

WHEN JT AWOKE MIDMORNING on Tuesday, he realized he needed more supplies—and not, for a change, because he'd let paint dry out or because he'd thrown a stylus against his studio wall. No, he was actually using the pigments and beeswax that had sat untouched for so long. Until recently, he'd considered the tubes and jars silently mocking, belligerent in their disuse. Now they seemed sad, neglected. JT felt repentant and eager to make up for lost time.

He hurried through brushing his teeth and threw on pants and a shirt that may or may not have technically matched. The sooner he got to the store and back, the sooner he could get to work.

He was still shoving his left foot into a sneaker as he opened the door to his apartment. Preoccupied as he was with half-formed plans for a treated piece of wood, it took him a moment to realize he was staring at the back of some guy. Not necessarily a notable event, except that the guy was standing in front of Kenzie's door, making no move to knock. He wore a pair of glasses, which he pushed up on his nose twice in less than a minute, muttering to himself the entire time. In his lightweight blazer and slacks, he looked like a well-dressed but slightly deranged encyclopedia salesman.

"Can I help you?" JT's voice came out more menacing than he'd intended, but he felt somewhat protective of Kenzie and her children.

The man jumped about a foot, then turned to face JT. He was older, by around a decade, JT guessed, and pale—a nervous potential suitor? After all, he didn't appear to have any encyclopedias, vacuums to demonstrate or literature inviting her to consider spiritual salvation. Then again, why court a woman in the middle of the workday? If he knew Kenzie, surely he realized she was at the bank now.

"I'm Dr. Forrest Smith," the man replied. He lifted his chin, a flinty gleam of determination showing behind the lenses of his wire-rim glasses. "And I'm here for my wife!"

"Oh." The guy was here for Ann, not Kenzie. Suddenly, JT liked him much better. "Well, good for you."

"Yes." Dr. Smith's shoulders slumped slightly. "She was. Maybe too good for me."

A mild and abstract kind of alarm pulsed through JT at the other man's confiding tone. Visions of that wood panel and his unrealized hopes for it fluttered through his subconscious. Still, neither the art store nor the wood were going anywhere, so he shoved his hands in his pockets and waited.

"Have you met Ann?" Dr. Smith asked.

"A couple of times. I don't know her well."

The other man was nodding absently, talking almost more to himself than JT. "She's younger than I am. I was surprised when she showed interest in me, but I got used to it. Used to her. She keeps everything so organized…."

If JT had just awakened half an hour sooner this morning, perhaps he would already be at the store, sorting through the—

"Are you good with women?" Dr. Smith asked suddenly.

"Hmm? Oh, no. Not really." What this guy needed was Sean, a natural-born charmer who never thought it was weird when total strangers asked him for opinions. JT wasn't charming, he was…isolated, awkward.

Although, holding Kenzie on the rooftop hadn't felt awkward. It had been instinctive and effortless, finding her mouth with his, kissing her as if he already knew her shape and taste and just how she liked to be caressed. Holding her against him, he sure as hell hadn't felt isolated.

Ann's husband was muttering again. "Damn, I should have brought flowers. I'm here to ask her to come home. Do you think I should have brought flowers with me? It would have been more romantic."

Truthfully, JT had no idea. He didn't know if Ann craved

romance or if she even intended to go home, though Kenzie seemed to think her sister's separation was temporary. Since this nervous-looking husband had asked for advice, JT spoke from his gut.

"I had a wife and child once. I'd give anything to spend another day with them. If you love your wife, tell her now. Stop dithering out in the hall, don't waste time going for flowers. Just. Tell. Her."

The man considered this, shoving his glasses up on the bridge of his nose in a move that was clearly more habit than necessity—they'd barely moved since the last time he'd pushed them into place. "Right. Right, why am I wasting time?" Without waiting for an answer, he pivoted and rapped sharply on the door.

JT hoped Ann and the baby weren't out running errands, or the results of her husband's resolve would be rather anti-climactic. JT breathed an inward sigh of relief when the door swung open. He was already turning to go when he heard a quizzical "Forrest?" from behind him. As he stepped inside the elevator, he glimpsed the embrace at the end of the hallway. From the way Ann was kissing her husband, he suspected she would indeed be going home soon.

JT averted his eyes quickly to give the couple more privacy, even though they were oblivious to his existence. Recalling Kenzie's nervousness about an audience the other day, he couldn't help wondering…what would have happened if they'd been alone when he kissed her? His blood heated at the thought, at the memory of her mouth.

What he'd told Forrest seemed like a split truth. JT would always hate the tragedy of Holly's death, that she'd sacrificed her life trying to give birth to the baby that hadn't made it, either. There had been plenty of days when he would have sold his own soul to spend five more minutes with her. Yet she hadn't haunted his dreams in the same way for months. While it would have felt disloyal to say it—even to himself—he knew he'd slowly been getting over her. This was more than simple healing, though. He was actively waking up with another woman's face and laugh and kiss on his mind. Kenzie had become the woman he wanted to spend time with.

She'd be gone soon, and part of him took comfort in that, a finite end rather than a shocking jolt.

After the wrenching double loss he'd suffered, he doubted he would ever again be capable of long-term emotional commitments…or that the wary single mother would even welcome one. Kenzie's moving would help them part ways naturally, without a lot of drama, and he welcomed the easy out. Still, he hoped to see her as much as possible before that happened.

JT KNEW IT WAS KENZIE BY the sound of her knock—light and quick as if she were both eager and shy. Or possibly, despite the open windows, he was strung out on paint fumes and turpentine.

"Just a sec," he called, cleaning his brush with a rag as he walked to the door.

As he'd expected, Kenzie, along with her son, who'd obviously changed out of his school clothes, waited on the other side. Drew wore denim cutoffs with ragged hems at the knee, a black T-shirt and a huge grin.

JT arched an eyebrow at him. "You look excited to get started."

"Yeah, I'm psyched. Leslie is torqued. Kept whining about how *she's* the one who—"

"Andrew." Kenzie squeezed his shoulder. "A little sensitivity, please. Remember your manners, or JT can punt you back to our apartment."

Frankly, JT was surprised the kid would rather be over here messing with art supplies instead of back home with his video games. Was it just the novelty of getting to do something that didn't include his sister? JT knew the boy's teachers thought he needed time around an adult male, but JT had a hard time seeing himself as a role model. Still, he was happy to help. Partly because he recalled the confused misery of his own adolescence…and, selfishly, because of the way Kenzie's eyes lit with gratitude. A look like that made a guy feel as if he could leap tall buildings in a single bound.

"Don't be too late," she added, and JT wasn't sure if the instruction was for him or Drew. "You promise you've finished your homework?"

"Yes, ma'am." If Drew didn't technically roll his eyes, it was implied in his tone.

"All right. But you still need to eat din—" She broke off, her gaze jerking up to meet JT's. "You should join us! I mean, if you want to. As a thank-you."

He couldn't help thinking of how she'd thanked him on a previous occasion. By the rosy flush climbing her cheeks, he guessed she was remembering the same thing. His eyes held hers, and if it hadn't been for Drew standing between them, JT would have leaned in to kiss her again. Her lips parted, and he forced himself to look away.

JT cleared his throat. "What time's dinner?"

"How about an hour?" she offered.

"Sure." When JT was in the creative zone, he could lose whole hours at a time, but he suspected that Drew would get bored long before then. An hour sounded reasonable for an actual art lesson, not that he was planning anything too formal.

He ushered Drew inside and began to give him a brief overview of paints. "As I told your sister, I do a lot of work with oils, but we probably won't start with that for you today. Acrylics are a fast-drying option, and watercolors don't involve much cleanup."

"Good," Drew said. "I don't like to clean."

"Artists have to take care of their equipment, though. There's a lot of discipline and hard work and routine involved. It's not just standing in front of an easel waiting for inspiration to strike and then breaking for a latte."

"Latte?" Drew wrinkled his nose. "That's a kind of coffee, right? Why would I want one of those?"

"Never mind. Let's round up some supplies and go up to the roof."

"You don't work in your apartment?"

"Sometimes I do, but a change of perspective can be good, not to mention the fresh air and natural light."

Drew trailed him to his studio, hanging back in the doorway as JT gathered some basic tools. "Thank you for letting me come over. I think Mom was nervous about asking you. She likes you, you know."

JT straightened, having no idea what the appropriate response was. Every time he looked at Kenzie, his temperature soared ten degrees, but he could hardly tell Drew that. "I like her, too." In fact, he liked the whole family a lot more than he would have thought possible in such a short time.

A disquieting acknowledgment. How much more emotionally invested would he become before it was time to bid them goodbye?

"Mom?" Leslie was supposed to be setting the table, but was instead leaning against the kitchen counter, getting under

Kenzie's feet as she tried to finish preparing dinner. "Are you okay? You look…kind of like I feel when I throw up."

Lovely. "I'm just busy, trying to get dinner ready." Although, if she *were* feeling the tiniest bit apprehensive about cooking for JT, it might be because a certain daughter had once tried to make her sound like Julia Child and Betty Crocker all rolled into one.

Kenzie was never going to be an award-winning chef, but she ought to be able to produce a decent-tasting, well-balanced meal. She had biscuits in the oven, chicken breasts in a pan with basil and white wine, and green beans boiling. *What am I forgetting?* Salad! She'd meant to put together a salad.

"Can you grab me carrots and a cucumber from the fridge? I'll chop, you wash lettuce leaves."

Leslie obliged. "You know," she said as she took the lettuce to the sink, "I would understand if you were feeling nauseous. My new friend Angel feels that way when she sees the boy she likes."

Aside from a twinge of motherly panic that girls Les's age were already noticing the opposite sex, Kenzie was relieved to hear Leslie casually mentioning friends—the kind that didn't exist solely in fiction. At least one of the twins was settling into the new school. "Maybe you could invite Angel over sometime."

"Cool. I bet she'll like the view from the roof. I like going up there to read and think," Leslie said. "I'll miss it when we move."

When they moved… Kenzie should take the kids for a drive by their future house this weekend. She could hardly recall what the place looked like. Oh, she had vague impressions, but the details were getting fuzzy. She needed the reminder that *that* was home, not Peachy Acres. Despite its cozy community feel and the neighbors she was getting to know, the complex was just a way station. Still, the apartment felt comfortably roomy with Ann and Abigail gone. Her sister had called Kenzie at the bank to say she and Forrest were going to work on resolving their problems—and that *he* was planning to cook an early dinner for *her*.

When the front door opened, Kenzie's heart thudded in anticipation. While she liked everyone she'd met in the building, there was no question that one neighbor in particular had become special to her.

Drew rushed in first, talking a mile a minute. "You want to see what I did? I used paper today, but JT said I could use canvas next time. I thought he was supposed to tell me what to draw or arrange a bowl of fruit or something, but he just gave me some colors and told me to go for it. He's a really lousy teacher."

Yet Drew was grinning from ear to ear and JT, entering the room behind him, wore a similar smile.

JT held his palms up in front of his body. "Hey, I never claimed to be a good instructor, kid. It's not my fault if you chose unwisely."

Leslie was peering at the paper in her brother's hand. "So, what is it?"

"I don't know yet. But remember some of those pictures we saw at the museum?" Drew adopted a pompous tone. "*Untitled in Yellow, Big Fat Splotch on Wood Circle.* JT said I can think about what the painting means to me, but that not all art has a... What was that word again?"

"*Literal?* Literal meaning?"

"Yeah! I'm gonna go wash my hands. When do we eat? I'm hungry."

"There's a surprise," Leslie muttered, obviously still put out that no one had invited *her* to come paint. Kenzie made a mental note to plan a fun mother-daughter activity the next time Drew went across the hall. Maybe if she and Les were giving each other pedicures and enjoying some boy-free quality time, her daughter would be less resentful.

"Something smells good in here," JT said. "Anything I can do to help?"

Kenzie smiled up at him. "No, that's—"

"You could set the table," Leslie said. "I was going to earlier, but then I came in here to calm Mom down."

"Calm her down?" He repeated the words to Leslie, but angled his questioning look at Kenzie.

Kenzie sliced a few more pieces of carrot, thinking with fond nostalgia of the days before the twins could speak. "Leslie, why don't *you* go set out the dishes, instead of trying to foist your chores off on our guest?"

"Okay." Lowering her voice to nowhere near a whisper as she passed, Leslie instructed her mother, "If you do feel nervous, you're supposed to take deep breaths. They're, like, soothing or something."

With a sardonic glance over her shoulder at the skillet, Kenzie reflected that perhaps the white wine would have been put to better use in a glass rather than in the chicken recipe.

JT came to stand next to her, leaning against the counter and clearly enjoying himself. "Anything I can do to help with your jittery nerves?"

Yes, go stand in the next room. But then she wouldn't be able to bask in his nearness, enjoy the unique smell of *him* that was noticeable beneath the astringent perfume of paint and whatever soap he used to scrub with after.

"My nerves are fine, thanks. My daughter, as you may have noticed, has an overactive imagination." Given the things Leslie had no compunction saying right in front of Kenzie, she shuddered to think what an unsupervised Drew might have said in the past hour. "So, how did it go?"

"Seemed okay. We sat on the roof, working on separate pieces. Every once in a while he'd ask my opinion or share something random from school. At first, he was tense whenever he thought he'd messed up. I explained that no stroke is wasted—sometimes the work goes in a different direction than you'd planned, but the very unexpectedness can be inspiring. It's always a learning experience, an exploration of sorts."

"I could listen to you talk about art all day. You have a way of making it sound interesting and personal."

"I could talk to you all day," he rejoined. "You make me feel more interesting than I am. What are you doing Friday night?"

"Uh, Friday?" she echoed, caught utterly off guard. "This Friday?"

"Yeah." He grinned, but a shadow of uncertainty passed in his gaze like the outline of a shark swimming just below the surface of the water. "Sean and I have been asked to a private gallery showing, with the invitation to bring guests, of course. I thought maybe you'd like to come with me and we could… talk about art some more."

Or kiss some more, thought the impulsive, undisciplined Kenzie. "*Yes.* Oh. No. I mean, it's kind of you to ask—"

"But you'd like to think about it?"

"Well, there are the kids to consider." Donning protective mitts, she sidestepped him to retrieve the biscuits from the oven. "I don't know if I can find a sitter in the next few days. Alicia comes by some afternoons, but she mentioned she's looking forward to the high school's first away game this weekend. Maybe Ann."

"She's gone, isn't she?" JT's tone was surprisingly satisfied. "Did she go back to her husband?"

"Apparently he came by today and swept her off her feet.

Or at least convinced her that he saw her as more than a glorified administrative assistant. They should be fine."

"Good. It's nice to see people get happy endings," he said softly, almost to himself.

As they all sat at the table, Kenzie kept replaying his words in her head.

Was it naive for people like her and JT, a divorcée and a widower, to believe in happy endings? That took a kind of pure-hearted faith she was afraid she'd outgrown. Still… She watched JT pass Drew the green beans and laugh at Leslie's imitation of Mrs. Kane. Vowing to call Ann first thing in the morning to ask about babysitting, Kenzie finally wrenched her gaze away from JT's handsome face.

Maybe she lacked the childlike optimism to believe in happy endings, but she couldn't help being seduced by the possibility of new beginnings.

Chapter Twelve

The surprise on Sean's face would have been comical if JT wasn't feeling so abashed. He was part owner of the gallery, yet how long had it been since he'd set foot here?

"Well, this is a red-letter event," his friend said, recovering. He took in JT's white shirt and jeans—the only pair he owned without obvious paint smears. "You even look halfway civilized. Wait, do I *know* you? For a second, I mistook you for someone else."

"Practicing for that career as a comedian in case the gallery closes?"

"Think I should put in a call to Punchline first, or the Funny Farm?"

Looking around, JT ignored the hypothetical question about Atlanta's comedy clubs. As far as he could tell, the two of them were the only people here. "*Is* the gallery in danger of closing?" He remembered how excited he, Sean and Holly had been when they first opened. JT shouldn't have neglected everything. He felt like a man coming out of a coma.

"No." Sean blinked. "I didn't mean to give you that impression. It's true that we made more of a profit when you were…"

"Painting?" His identity as an artist was supposed to have lent the gallery cachet.

"More active in the art community, I was going to say. We still get customers. You just came at a slow time."

"Well, I come with good news." JT shoved his hands in his pockets, wanting to share his joy but not wanting to make more of it than it was. After all, a few colorful blotches did not a career reinvention make. "I, uh, started a painting."

Sean's eyes widened, but he kept his tone casual. "Yeah?"

"Yeah. I mean, it's not entirely right. I may scrap it and take another stab, but…it felt good."

His friend let out an excited whoop. "This is fantastic! We'll celebrate this weekend. You want me to call Whitney and see if she has a friend free on Friday? We could double."

"About that…" He hesitated. "I invited Kenzie to the showing."

Sean's jaw dropped. "Wow. I knew you liked her, but I didn't think you were ready to take the next step. I'm proud of you, man."

JT squirmed. "It's not that big a deal. I like her company, so I asked her to join us."

"Not that big a deal? Isn't she the reason you're painting again? The reason you're out and about in clothes that don't look like they came out of a rag bin?"

"No." *Maybe.* "So I did some laundry. It was time."

"Way past." Sean rounded the short, curved counter to clap his friend on the shoulder. "Whatever spurred you, I'm glad to have you back, buddy. Tell Kenzie I look forward to seeing her Friday night."

"She hasn't actually said yes yet. She needed to look for a sitter."

"Ah, right. Brave of you, getting involved with a mom. I love my nieces and nephews, but still…"

JT rolled his eyes. "'Involved'? It's one night in a group setting. You have a more overactive imagination than Leslie."

"Le—?" Sean stopped short. "Did you just compare me to Kenzie's kid?"

The words had just popped out, but JT was still adjusting to having the Greens in his building, much less cropping up in his everyday conversation. "You should be flattered. Kenzie has great kids."

Sean started laughing then, barely managing to stop long enough to gasp, "Oh, yeah, you're not *involved* at all."

JT gave him a one-finger salute and decided his time was better spent back at the apartment, working on his painting, than dealing with the mockery of his so-called friend.

At home, he put in a CD of a local rock band he liked, and changed into a T-shirt and jeans that were more paint than denim. Then he dived into work, losing all track of time until he was distracted by a knock at the door. Jarred out of his creative flow, he swore under his breath, then realized guiltily that his music was probably too loud. He hit Stop and answered the door. Instead of finding Mr. C. with a noise complaint, he found Kenzie, looking beautiful and shy.

"H-hi." Her smile was tentative. "Am I interrupting?"

"Not at all." He followed her gaze to the small splatters that had accumulated on his hands and clothes in the past few hours. "Okay, you caught me. I was definitely working—I'd hate for you to think I look like this all the time—but it's no bother. What can I do for you?"

She lowered her eyes. "You've already done so much. Even when he was getting ready for school this morning, Drew was talking my ear off about ideas he has for possible artwork. And trust me, Drew is *not* a morning person."

Was she? JT wondered. He couldn't stop himself from imagining how Kenzie woke up in the morning. Refreshed from sleep, did she rise efficient and ready to tackle the day? Or was she softer, dreamier? That was a Kenzie he'd like to see.

There was also the possibility that she woke up as cranky as a bear, but he suspected she could make even that adorable.

"JT?"

"Mmm?"

"Your mind's still on your painting," she guessed apologetically. "I won't keep you. I just wanted to let you know that I talked to Ann today. She said she'll pick the kids up from school on Friday, and they can spend the night with her."

She blushed as soon as she'd finished the sentence, and JT raised an eyebrow.

"In case it's a late night," she added hurriedly. "We don't have to worry about getting back at any p-particular time."

"Right. That makes sense." But didn't explain the blush. He grinned inwardly. "Tell your sister I owe her one."

She nodded. "Will do. I, ah, guess I'll see you Friday."

"It's a date." Belatedly, he recalled saying those words to her once before and getting blasted with an automatic disclaimer.

This time, however, she didn't disagree. Instead, she sank her teeth into the full lower lip he suddenly couldn't stop staring at. Though she looked a bit skittish, her eyes sparked with the blue fire of excitement, too. As if she wouldn't mind his kissing her again.

Before he did exactly that, she gave herself a slight shake and smiled at him. "It's a date."

THE WOMAN WITH THE LOOSE curls and black dress appeared so different from the one who went to work at the bank every day that Kenzie almost panicked when she heard the knock at the door. *I should change! JT can't see me like this.* He was perceptive enough to take one look and know she was a fraud, a harried single mom impersonating someone glamorous.

Too bad Leslie wasn't home tonight to allay her fashion fears. Kenzie alternated between elation at not having to worry about any unwanted witnesses for a good-night kiss, and sheer terror. While she'd never consciously used her children as a shield against romantic entanglements, they'd certainly created a buffer.

Tonight, bufferless and wearing such a comparatively short skirt, she felt naked. Which did nothing to help her regain her composure as she opened the door.

She forced a smile. "H— Mick!"

Her ex-husband's wide brown eyes were filled with only slightly less surprise than she was feeling. "Mackenzie. Wow, look at you. *Nice.*" His gaze swept down her form in frank appreciation.

There was a time in her life when getting that look from him would have weakened her knees, but when she recalled her reaction now, it was so distant that it felt like seeing someone else's memories rather than experiencing her own.

His grin was crooked as he teased, "Didn't have to get all dressed up on my account."

"How could I have when I had no idea you were coming?" Her date was scheduled to arrive in a few minutes, and here stood her ex-husband. She was hard-pressed to imagine a more awkward social situation.

"I told you I wanted it to be a surprise!" He looked so damn pleased with himself that she wanted to scream.

Even if he'd been trying to do something sweet, did he ever think about the three of them? Understand that they had lives of their own and weren't just sitting around waiting for him to have an opening in his schedule?

"You gave me the address in case I wanted to send the kids anything, so I looked you up on the Internet," he continued. "Where are the they, by the way? I've got presents for them both."

She started to shove her hands through her hair until she remembered how much trouble she'd gone to with the curling iron, then gritted her teeth instead. "It's nice that you came to see them, and I'm sure they'll be thrilled to know gifts are involved, but they aren't here. They're with my sister and won't be back until tomorrow."

He grimaced. "They're with Annie? Well, they aren't going to have any fun with that sourpuss. Why don't I—"

"Ann's not a sourpuss. She was just always mature for her age." *Which is more than I can say for some of us.*

"I still think the kids would have more fun with their dad tonight. Come on, Mac, I'm not going to be in town long, and—"

"Of course you're not!" She threw her hands in the air. "Mick, they're not toddlers anymore. They aren't content to giggle while you tickle them for twenty minutes, then wave slobbery fists goodbye when you leave. Again. They're old enough to ask questions, to want explanations—from *me,* thank you very much—about why you can't keep the most basic promises, why you can't be relied on to send freaking birthday cards. They're twins—you only have to remember one date."

His posture had turned defensive, his jaw clenched. "I'm here now, aren't I? I'm trying. I told you I was working to change, and all you can do is bust my chops about the past?"

She sagged in the doorway, wanting to kick off her high heels and spend the rest of the night hiding in her room within the folds of a comfy robe. "I get that you're trying. I applaud you for it. But I will not rearrange this family's plans to make life more convenient for you. I tried to tell you when we got divorced—it can't always be about you, not when you're a parent."

His gaze, scathing this time, raked over her again. "Fairly self-righteous coming from a woman who got rid of her kids for the night and looks ready to—"

"If you finish that sentence, I will slap you."

He reddened.

As well he should. Even when they'd been married, he'd flirted with band groupies and women at nightclubs. Before the kids had been born Kenzie had always been there to keep a proprietary eye on him, indulging him as he winked at females who would hopefully go on to buy his CDs. But swollen to three times her normal size in the eighth month of pregnancy, and later at home with crying infants, she'd had the occasional stab of insecurity about his faithfulness. It was a question she'd never brought herself to ask as their marriage ended—what would be the point when she was already bitter over so many other issues? She liked to think he'd never strayed, but after the divorce, he sure as hell hadn't been celibate, and had no right to require it of her.

Not that she'd already decided to sleep with JT!

No, it was just the principle of… Suddenly she was too distracted by hazy but provocative images to complete her thought. She fanned her face with her hand.

"I apologize," Mick said formally. "I was being an ass. Whoever he is, he's lucky to have you. You were always my biggest fan, and I screwed it up. I'm sorry I hurt you."

"Don't worry about me. Worry about your children. It's not too late, Mick. Don't screw things up with them."

"I—" He broke off, both of them turning as JT came out of his own apartment, looking incredible in black slacks and a lightweight black turtleneck.

Very sophisticated, very sexy. A giggle welled up in her throat as she considered her own all-black ensemble. Together, they would look like a pair of overdressed cat burglars.

JT had drawn up short, noticing Mick, but flashed Kenzie a warm smile. "Sorry, I lost track of time painting. Any man who keeps a woman like you waiting should be shot."

"Thank you. But let's forgo the firearms. Buy me a drink, we'll call it even."

Next to JT, Mick suddenly looked older, even though the two men couldn't be far apart in age. Still, there was something haggard in her ex-husband's face—too little sleep, too many late-night sessions fuelled by alcohol and nicotine. He stuck a hand out in her date's direction. "Mick Green."

JT's expression was inscrutable as he shook his hand. "Jonathan Trelauney."

Glancing back at her, Mick managed a smile that looked at least half-sincere. "You two have fun tonight. I'll…call you tomorrow morning about seeing the kids."

"That would be good." Feeling strangely melancholy, she watched him stride down the hall and disappear into the elevator.

He was making a renewed effort, which as a mom she appreciated, and nothing had changed between them in years— she was more than free to date—so why did she feel sad? *Pity.* She felt sorry for the man who'd lost his family in pursuit of a dream, only to eventually lose even that.

"Hey." JT reached out, lightly cupping the side of her face. "You all right?"

She nodded wordlessly.

"We could alter our plans if you want, maybe stay in.

Although that would be a *huge* sacrifice on my part. As you may have noticed, I'm quite the crowd-loving extrovert."

In spite of her mood, she giggled. "That's the very first thing I noticed about you."

He leaned closer. "Would you like to know the first thing I noticed about *you,* Kenzie?"

"I'm not sure."

"Proportion is important to an artist, ratio and dimensions and the different ways to manipulate them. And you seemed out of proportion, with so much life and spirit in such a relatively small frame. Although the frame is quite nice." He trailed his gaze over her face, collarbone, the straps of her dress and the hint of cleavage below, then back to meet her eyes. "You steal my breath, the way you try to be stern but then smile. You have a great smile."

"So do you." She reached out to trace his lips with her finger. "I wish I saw it more."

Capturing her hand, he pressed a featherlight kiss to her palm. "I can guarantee I've smiled more since I met you than in the entire past year."

A flattering comment, but she wasn't sure she wanted the responsibility for making him smile. Seeing Mick tonight had reminded her of her former role as a cheerleader. Supporting his artistic dream and cajoling him out of moody doubts when a song wasn't coming together or a purported talent scout didn't show had required nearly as much effort and energy as raising twin babies. Barely an adult herself, she hadn't had it in her to nurture all three of them without losing her own sanity. She was more stable now, the children less mindlessly demanding, but she didn't want to carry the burden of someone else's happiness.

At least, not on a long-term basis.

Right now, JT's complimentary gaze and deadpan jokes were making her happy, and she hoped to return the favor. She had one whole night free to selfishly spend on herself, and she planned to devote the evening to their mutual pleasure.

"CAN I GET YOU ANOTHER glass of wine, Kenzie?" JT offered, one hand resting comfortably at the small of her back.

Before she could answer, Sean grumbled good-naturedly, "Better let me get it. At least that'll give me something to do besides stand here like a third wheel."

Earlier, Sean had told Kenzie how thrilled he'd been to learn she was joining them. Unfortunately, his own date had canceled because of a cold. Before this evening, Kenzie couldn't remember ever being so pleasantly spoiled. She was accompanied by not one but two handsome men who possessed tons of knowledge about art as well as senses of humor. They'd kept her thoroughly entertained as they squired her through the small upscale gallery, studying photographs and sculptures. In fact, they were so solicitous and charming she feared the attention was going to her head. She felt unnaturally light, nearly giddy.

"I think I should pass on a second wine," she said. She'd noted that JT had stuck solely to soft drinks all evening. "But thank you."

"Well, I'm going to get myself some refreshment," Sean said, the twinkle in his gaze belying his gloomy tone. "At least *pretend* to notice my absence."

JT grinned at Kenzie. "Did you hear something?"

She elbowed him gently. "You're going to wound his ego. He's very delicate."

Sean snorted. "I don't have to stand here and take this abuse. I can go get plenty of abuse on the other side of the room."

As his friend walked away, JT chuckled with wry admiration. "He'll probably end up with some pretty woman at the bar buying him a drink to make up for the way his friends are ignoring him."

"So his date tonight wasn't a girlfriend?"

"No. Sean's a great guy, but he doesn't have a lot of interest in long-term romantic relationships."

"I can understand that," Kenzie said without thinking.

JT cocked his head. "My experience is limited, but usually women cluck their tongues and say that settling down would be healthier for him."

"Maybe it would. But that's not everyone's experience, is it?"

"No," he replied softly.

They both turned back to the framed black-and-white photograph in front of them, but there was only so long they could pretend to be studying its unique focus on the background, instead of the deliberately blurred subject in the center of the shot.

"Did it upset you to see your ex tonight?" JT asked. "You've been a really good sport about being here."

"A rare night on the town with two guys who keep me laughing? Yeah, that's a hardship." She squeezed his hand. "I wasn't upset. His unannounced presence just threw me at first. He thought it would be fun for the kids if he surprised them."

"And you don't agree?"

"I wish he'd think about more than 'fun.' He's been the glamorous parent, the one off in a band who shows up for a few hours without sticking around for middle-of-the-night flu or teacher conferences. I'm the one worrying about homework and orthodontist visits and bills—all the daily grind that isn't sexy."

"Don't sell yourself short." JT's expression took on an

almost predatory gleam that was both disconcerting and thrilling. "Even in day-to-day routine, you're plenty sexy."

She lowered her eyes. "Flatterer."

He shook his head. "I watched you put away dishes in your kitchen, the way your clothes slid and clung to the curves of your body. I openly ogled as you popped a bite of warm, buttery biscuit between your lips."

For a man who made a living evoking emotion visually, he was pretty skilled verbally, too. He had the ability to wring powerful reactions from her without even touching her. Which was kind of a shame—she really, really wanted him to touch her. The desire had grown throughout the night into a sweet-sharp craving she saw no reason to deny.

Her throat felt so dry it was hard to get words out. "So, um, how much longer do you think we should stay?"

"Why, you tired?" There was a silky, teasing note in his voice.

"Ready to go someplace more intimate," she corrected.

She looked around in search of Sean. They'd arrived in separate cars, but it only seemed polite to bid him farewell. Raising his hand above the rest of the crowd, JT waved for Sean's attention and made their goodbye by pointing toward the exit as he ushered Kenzie through the room. Ten minutes later, they were on the road. Although he was driving at a nice, safe speed—below the limit, by Atlanta's standards—Kenzie felt as if she were hurtling toward something overwhelming and inevitable.

And she couldn't wait to get there.

Chapter Thirteen

In an endearing gentlemanly fashion, JT quickly got out of the car and rushed around to open her door. The September night was still warm enough to be muggy. To Kenzie, it felt as if even the air was throbbing and heavy with expectation. He took her hand, and, dazed, she let him lead her inside the building.

The elevator doors slid apart to admit them. For a change, Sylvia Myer wasn't present with her button-pushing daughter. *Must be after the little girl's bedtime.* Tonight, Kenzie and JT were all alone. A wave of wanting swamped her, and she watched him hungrily.

As soon as the elevator jolted into motion, he reached for her. His arms, bands of gentle steel, encircled her in a fierce embrace. Ducking to her height, he claimed her mouth, absorbing her breathy gasp. Had she ever wanted a man so intensely?

The elevator halted. *Thank goodness.* Somewhere in the course of the evening—perhaps when he'd first made her laugh after Mick's departure, or when he'd held open the gallery door, or when he'd told her how sexy she was—she'd subconsciously reached the decision to make love with him. But she needed to get him into one of their apartments before she had time to lose her nerve.

As they neared the end of the hallway, JT asked, "Should I walk you home, or do you want to come over for a little while?"

"I'd like to see your place." She'd never made it past the threshold.

He'd barely ushered her inside before he pressed her against the wall, kissing her with even more fervor than in the elevator. He nipped at her bottom lip, saying between kisses, "I'm...a lousy...host." Pulling back slightly, he trailed a hand over the side of her neck, toward the modest swell of cleavage revealed by her dress. "I should offer you a drink or something."

She tilted her head back, arching toward his touch. "I'll take the 'or something.'"

When he kissed her again, she could feel the smile on his lips. They took their time, necking like a couple of teenagers. There was no doubt in Kenzie's mind that he wanted her as desperately as she wanted him, but they had the whole night ahead of them. The sensual side of her appreciated the tantalizing foreplay; the part of her that was nervous about having sex for the first time in years was grateful for the slow seduction.

Finally they drew apart and JT chuckled wryly. "I really am a bad host. The least I could do was find a more comfortable spot. We could move to the couch?"

Or the bed. Was that too forward? "Actually, could you show me around? I'd love to see where you work."

"All right."

His floor plan was a lot different than hers. Where the space in her apartment was carved up for a maximum number of rooms and vanity nooks, his was considerably more open. The living room was larger, flowing into the kitchen, with very little separation except the breakfast bar divider. There was a single bathroom and two bedrooms, one of which he'd converted into a studio. His apartment looked recently cleaned, not as messy as she would have expected from a bachelor.

The studio was fascinating. There were several easels set up, small electric tools she didn't recognize sitting atop a square table, shelving units full of paint and other supplies placed against the walls. Some sort of respiratory mask hung right beneath the light switch. Everything clearly had a place…except for the art itself, which was scattered everywhere. A large piece of wood lay on a window seat, half its surface covered in colors and waxy texture, and on the floor below were wadded-up pieces of sketching paper. Old canvases were stacked in a corner, and one had slid off the pile. The surface of a desk had disappeared entirely under an inch-thick layer of drawings. There was a palpable energy in the room; she could easily picture his artistic mania, JT sketching and muttering to himself as he tried to produce just the right image.

Kenzie glanced around, taking it all in. "How long have you been— Oh!" Her gaze fell on a picture that lay crookedly across a chair.

He quickly moved between her and the object she was studying. "How long have I been painting, you were going to ask?"

"Was that picture of *me?*"

He shot her a helpless look, obviously embarrassed that she'd spotted it.

"Can I see it?"

"It's not very good. My work is more abstract by nature. It's difficult for me to accurately capture a real person."

A grin tugged at her lips—he sounded like her kids when they were stalling. "Please?"

"Here. Don't say I didn't warn you."

She took a step closer to reach for the paper, and their fingers brushed. The fleeting contact gave her a warm *zing,* but it was nothing compared to the dizzying sensation that went through her when she looked at the picture.

"Good heavens," she breathed. "Is this… This is how you see me?"

Earlier that evening, she'd looked at her own reflection and felt a jolt of fractured identity, knowing the woman she saw was Kenzie Green, yet in many ways not recognizing her. Seeing JT's drawing was similar, only a hundred times more powerful. She didn't think her mouth was really that sensual. And she was amazed at how expressive the eyes were even without color. Despite his modest claim about not capturing people well, he'd done a phenomenal job.

He'd focused mainly on her face, her hair a smudgy free-form impression of loose waves on the edges of the picture. Thank God he hadn't drawn her body. She didn't think she could take the effect of seeing that.

She glanced up with amazement, meeting his nervous gaze. "This is beautiful."

"I was depicting a subject who's beautiful."

It was on the tip of her tongue to protest that she wasn't that beautiful, not really, but he was there, kissing her, before she could.

She'd expected a studio to smell more like the paints she'd had occasion to use over the years, mostly poster paint or spray paint, but it was difficult to describe the sweet scent permeating the room. Earthy and ripe. Between the aroma, the colors and textures and most of all the man who held her cradled against him, standing in JT's studio was the most pleasurable assault on her senses she'd ever encountered. As he kissed her, he traced lazy patterns up and down both her shoulders, stopping at the top to fiddle with the straps of her dress.

His voice was nearly hoarse. "Maybe I could show you the rest of the apartment now?"

The only part left was his bedroom. "Yes."

When they reached his room, instead of flicking the light switch, he crossed the dim interior and turned on a lamp—a delicate-looking stained-glass piece.

"Pretty," she said. The riot of illuminated colors reminded her of the mural he'd done for the museum.

"Thank you." He studied the fixture. "I just recently pulled it out of storage to give the room more life."

She took a guess. "Was it your wife's?"

"She gave it to me for Valentine's Day one year." He glanced up with a rueful smile. "This is inappropriate, isn't it, standing here with my gorgeous date and talking about Holly?"

"You loved her. That makes you the man you are…a man I'm extremely attracted to. Acknowledging the woman you shared your life with doesn't bother me."

"Thank you. Let me show you the other thing I rescued from storage." He pointed to the left, at a segmented painting that was clearly one work but took place over three different panels.

"Yours?" Unlike the children's mural, there was no clear image in this, but it was a rich mass of reds and violets in broad, lush strokes. Though not graphic, it was indefinably erotic.

"Mmm. One of my earlier pieces. It was featured in a magazine once, and I had offers to buy. At the time, I was so proud of it and so afraid that I might not produce anything else quite as good that I refused to let go."

"It's fantastic." She crossed the room for a better look, hearing his footsteps, smelling his cologne, as he approached. At the first touch of his lips against her bare shoulder, she shivered with anticipation. He pressed a kiss to the nape of her neck, then traced the shell of her ear with his mouth. She moved restlessly against him, ultimately turning in his arms so that she had better access.

She meshed her fingers in his hair. "You make me so… I haven't felt like this in a long time."

After that, neither of them spoke. The only sounds were of their mingled breathing, whispers of fabric as clothes brushed against each other or were removed, and muffled jazz from the apartment below. JT was adept enough at keeping her in a sensual haze that Kenzie didn't get nervous when her dress pooled at her ankles. Besides, she was preoccupied with removing his shirt. It wasn't the first time she'd seen his quite impressive naked chest, but before, she hadn't been free to touch him. Now, she trailed her fingers over the flat muscular planes and the modest dusting of dark hair. Warm male flesh. She'd seen beautiful sculptures of the human form before, but no matter how masterfully rendered, cold marble would always be vastly inferior to the original subject.

Not until JT reached behind her to find the clasp of her bra did real apprehension ripple through her.

He must have sensed her infinitesimal withdrawal because he stopped immediately. "Am I rushing you? We don't have—"

"No, everything you're doing is perfect." The thought of him seeing her body wasn't nearly as daunting as the prospect of his no longer touching her.

Her breasts were aching. Taking control of the moment and banishing her own timidity, she unfastened the bra and shrugged, letting the lacy black material fall. His expression turned to one of near reverence, a supremely gratifying reaction from a big, strapping man like JT.

He ran his thumb along the swell of one breast, curving to

the sensitive underside in a lazy circle, tracing smaller and smaller spheres until he finally brushed the peak with the pad of his thumb. Her eyes closed involuntarily, and her legs trembled with the effort to remain standing. He cupped both her breasts, then dropped his hands to her satin-covered backside, pulling her closer for another soul-searing kiss.

Desire quaked inside her, leaving her weak and breathless. She clung to him. "JT." Was that her voice? The husky rasp sounded like a commercial for an adult phone line.

He kissed her throat again, his fingers continuing their exquisite ministrations across her breasts. "I'm right here, sweetheart." Taking her hand, he tugged her gently toward the bed.

Kenzie sank into the mattress, savoring his weight atop her, squirming at the feel of him so close to where she most wanted him. He moved away to shuck the pants he'd been wearing, and her mouth went dry at the sight of him in formfitting boxer briefs. *Oh, my.* She was a very lucky girl. If her body wasn't throbbing with such excruciating pleasure, she might even be a little nervous at the thought of this man inside her.

He didn't allow her much time to think, however. Bending his head over her, a dark contrast to her pale breasts, he drew a nipple into the damp heat of his mouth. Even though she enjoyed every touch, she could have sobbed in relief when he finally retrieved a condom from the nightstand drawer. She tilted her hips, helping to guide him, and gasped at the sensation. For a moment, neither of them moved, and she met his eyes, the visual connection somehow as intimate as being physically joined.

Then he began to thrust in long, slow strokes, and Kenzie's breath became uneven as she responded with answering movements. He braced himself with one hand, keeping the other entwined with hers on the quilt next to her head. She squeezed his fingers, nearly writhing as delicious spasms built deep within her and radiated through her limbs, from the top of her head to the tips of toes curled in satisfaction. At the end, she cried out in wordless ecstasy, and JT crushed her against him, murmuring against her hair.

Kenzie's heart was racing so hard she expected it to fly free of her chest. For a brilliantly colored, suspended moment in time, her entire body had felt that way—free of all worries and soaring.

She licked her lips. "That…that was…" So much for being articulate. But who could blame her for not being one hundred percent coherent after the most powerful climax of her life?

"Agreed." They lay there in a sweaty, contented tangle for a few more minutes before he attempted to speak again. "Stay tonight?"

She nodded. Right now, there was no place in the world she'd rather be.

"Mmm." Eyes closed, Kenzie moaned in bliss. "Lord, this is good."

"Careful." JT, shirtless and grinning, shot her a completely ineffective look of reprimand. "I'm going to think you get more pleasure out of the enchiladas than the sex. Horrible for my self-esteem."

She giggled. "No disrespect to Mrs. Sanchez's cooking, but the sex was definitely the high point of the evening."

He regarded her with a skeptically raised eyebrow. "Are you just saying that to get another bite?"

"Maybe." She tucked the sheet more firmly around her and reached for the fork in his hand. After making love earlier, they'd cuddled in sleepy contentment until Kenzie admitted she was starving. She'd forgotten just how energetic sex could be, and it seemed to have revved up her appetite. Of course, there was also the fact that she'd been so nervous earlier in the day about her date with JT that she'd barely eaten.

So he'd microwaved a plate of leftovers and brought it back to bed with a couple of chilled bottles of water.

I'm lounging in bed, being fed by a half-naked man who has the body of a Greek god. Did life get any better?

He swallowed his own bite of food and smiled. "And to think I was aloof to Mrs. Sanchez the first few times she came by."

"Aloof? A people person like you?"

He reached around to swat her on the fanny. "You're not allowed to hang out with Sean anymore. I see his sarcasm is wearing off on you."

She laughed. "But I like Sean. I had so much fun tonight." Truthfully, when JT was relaxed, he was every bit as humorous as his friend. It was a thrill to see him playful and happy. "Were you…"

"Was I what?" he prompted.

But her mouth had been running faster than her thoughts and she winced now at what she'd been about to ask. "I was just…thinking…about what you might have been like in the past."

He studied her for a minute. "You mean when Holly was alive?"

Kenzie nodded, hoping she wasn't casting a pall over the moment. "When you met her. You were probably less, as you put it, aloof then." If he'd flashed that devastating smile often, his late wife had probably fallen in love within moments. If Kenzie wasn't careful…

"Actually, I was always fairly guarded. I didn't come from a very demonstrative family, and the emotions my parents *did* demonstrate didn't leave me eager to open up to anyone. I didn't think I had much emotion to offer, except through my paintings."

The first few times she'd met him, Kenzie might have agreed. Now she knew better. He was a man who cared—and hurt—deeply.

"I know I wasn't the world's best boyfriend or husband, but she put up with me." He ran a finger along Kenzie's jaw. "She would have liked you."

"Thank you." Kenzie was touched, knowing she'd been paid a very special compliment.

Their gazes locked, and Kenzie felt longing swirl through her. Not just physical longing—although that was there, too— but the longing to erase any pain he'd ever suffered, the longing to show him how much he had to offer, and prove to herself that despite her post-divorce cynicism, she, too, had a lot to give another person.

Like what? Love? It wasn't a question she wanted to face right now. So instead, she stole the last bite of enchilada, eliciting a mock growl of protest from JT.

"There are going to be consequences for that, woman."

With a shriek, she came off the bed. "Should I make a run for it?"

"You could." He grinned. "But I plan to catch you."

She'd never looked forward to facing consequences so much in her life. Yet as the two of them laughed and wrestled, a tiny part of her heart warned that, sooner or later, there would be emotional consequences, too.

Chapter Fourteen

Huddled in a borrowed sweatshirt that fell past midthigh, Kenzie stood at the large window in JT's living room. Streaks of burnt orange and scarlet had appeared on the horizon and were slowly streaking across the early dawn sky in a beautiful blossom of color, but she couldn't help resenting the sunrise. Her magical night with JT was at an end.

The wafting aroma of coffee preceded his footsteps. A moment later, he joined her. She gratefully accepted the mug he offered.

He lifted his chin toward the window. "Gorgeous, isn't it?"

"I guess."

"You *guess?*" He laughed, kissing the side of her neck. "You're definitely tough enough to be an art critic."

She ran her fingers over his stubbled jaw. "I'll need to leave soon."

No matter how much she wanted to spend the next few hours lounging in JT's bed, she needed to get in touch with Ann first thing this morning and arrange to pick up the twins before Mick called. While Kenzie had refused to change everyone's plans last night to accommodate his surprise arrival, she didn't want to deprive her kids of spending whatever time possible with him before he left again.

JT rested his head on top of hers. "Let me make you breakfast first? You're probably famished."

"True," she said with a grin. She should be exhausted, too, but up until she'd seen those first rays of sun, she'd felt invigorated, buzzing with excitement and life. She hadn't had a night with so little sleep since the twins were babies.

After the late-night enchiladas, she and JT had showered. Eventually they'd made love again, a slow, sweet union that left Kenzie glad there'd been no men in her life for years, that she'd waited for this one very special man. JT was a night person used to being up during the wee hours, but he'd insisted she try to sleep. Instead they'd wound up talking for hours. In the intimate darkness, he'd told her candidly about selling the house he'd shared with his wife, and coming to Peachy Acres, where he'd begun to heal. Kenzie told him about her own upcoming move and the Perfect Home. Yet even as he said the house she was buying sounded wonderful, she'd been assailed by unexpected misgivings.

Living here had spoiled her in some ways. She'd had more help and more time with the kids. Once she moved, there'd be an increased commute, plus weekend hours that would be eaten up by lawn and garden maintenance. There would be no companionable meals with Mrs. Sanchez. And what would Kenzie do when a gasket blew or a fuse shorted? In Raindrop, if a repair job outstripped her own skills, she'd known who to trust for affordable assistance. Here, she'd relied on Mr. C. whenever there was a problem. Even though she'd only been here a short time, she'd miss the people.

Especially this one, she thought, staring into JT's eyes.

"Hey." He touched her cheek. "You okay?"

No. Suddenly, she wasn't. "Can I get a rain check on that meal together? I appreciate the generous offer. I just…"

"Need to go." He stepped away.

"JT, thank you for last night. It was extraordinary." Choking back the lump of emotion in her throat, she held up her still-full mug. "And thanks for the coffee, too."

"Feel free to take that with you," he said.

"I'll, uh, just return the cup later," she promised. After he'd seen and touched most of her exposed body, would it be awkward to run into him? To pass him in the hall or bring Drew by for painting lessons? *Not that I'll be here much longer to run into him.* Which was for the best. Even knowing they weren't right for each other in the long range, Kenzie's heart might get different ideas if she remained in JT's proximity for an extended period.

"Sure." He gave her a sad, understanding smile, making no move to touch her. "You know where to find me."

THE TENSION IN Kenzie's apartment was so crushing that she expected light fixtures to start shattering at random. *Mick, if you don't call, I will hunt you down and beat you to death with your own guitar.* Or, at the very least, give him a really strongly worded piece of her mind.

Despite being tired, she'd dutifully crossed town to pick up the kids at Ann's that morning. On the way home, she'd shared with them the good news that their dad was nearby and wanted to spend some time with them. Lunchtime had passed hours ago, and still no word from her ex.

After pushing away an uneaten sandwich and declaring himself not hungry, Drew had gone to his room, punctuating his retreat with a slammed door. It was the kind of behavior Kenzie would normally reprimand. Today, she had neither the heart to chide him nor the energy. Leslie, predictably, had curled up on the couch and sought escape in a book. Kenzie couldn't help noticing her daughter hadn't turned a page in a long time.

Kenzie sat down and scooped her daughter's feet into her lap. It seemed only yesterday Kenzie had been playing "This Little Piggy" with tiny baby feet. Now Leslie painted her toes neon colors and wore shoes only a few sizes smaller than her mom. "You want to talk about it?"

"My book? Sure. It's a mystery," Leslie began. "There's this girl named Turtle who—"

"I meant about your dad," Kenzie clarified, even though she was pretty sure her daughter already knew that. "You must be disappointed."

Leslie affected a nonchalant shrug. "Not really."

"This is partly my fault," Kenzie said, second-guessing her selfish impulse to spend last night with JT. "Your dad came by last night, but you were already at Aunt Ann's. I should've—"

"We had fun there," Leslie interrupted. "We made cookies and I got to help give Abby a bath. It's way easier at their house than it was here because there's more space. And Uncle Forrest showed us a computer game that uses math. It's kind of hard, but Drew figured it out better than I did."

Kenzie's heart squeezed with gratitude, even as her eyes filled with tears. *She* was supposed to be comforting her daughter, yet, mature beyond her nine years, Leslie had reversed their roles. "Thank you, honey."

"You're a good parent," Leslie said fiercely. She hugged her mom, but a moment later pulled away, looking sheepish. "I mean, at least you didn't give us goofy names like Turtle or anything."

Kenzie ruffled the girl's hair. "Well, I *was* thinking of Salamander for you, but changed my mind at the last minute."

Chuckling, Leslie returned to her book. *One down.* Now, to deal with the other....

Armed with napkins and a handful of Drew's favorite cookies, Kenzie knocked on his door. "Can I come in?"

"'Kay."

It was worse than she'd anticipated. He wasn't even angrily crashing toy cars into each other or blowing something up via handheld video game. He was merely lying on his bed, scowling at the ceiling.

"I brought you some chocolate-chip cookies," she said coaxingly.

"You never let us eat dessert if we don't eat nutritious food first."

"Well, today I'm making an exception."

"Because of Dad," he said flatly.

"Because you're my son and I love you and I thought you could use a little cheering up." When he didn't reach for the cookies she was offering, she placed them on the nightstand and sat next to him. "Your dad really wanted to see you last night."

"Sure he did."

"Did you understand when I was explaining about his changing jobs? He's trying a different path that will hopefully allow more time for you and Leslie. Maybe he got busy with one of his clients today and plans to call us later."

Drew glared. "So these clients are more important than us?"

"Of course not!" Kenzie stifled further thoughts of homicide and tried to get her foot out of her mouth. "It's just that—"

Mercifully, she was interrupted by the ringing phone. She jumped off the bed. "I'll bet that's him now!"

"Yippee," her son intoned.

By the time Kenzie returned to the living room, Leslie had already answered. Her daughter glanced up with wide eyes. "It's

Dad!" She said it with the same wonder as if she'd just discovered Santa Claus setting out presents Christmas morning.

"That's wonderful, honey." Kenzie held out her hand. "Do you mind if I speak to him for a minute?"

Leslie nodded. "Mom wants to talk to you…. Okay, see you soon!" She hopped off the sofa, passing the phone over before running down the hall to share the news with Drew.

"Mick." Kenzie bit down all greetings along the lines of *what the hell took you so long* and kept her tone even. "I'm glad you got a chance to call. I have to confess, I thought we would hear from you earlier in the day."

"Well, I wanted to make sure I wasn't disrupting anyone's plans," he said caustically.

Be the bigger person, Kenzie. "Everyone's here now, no set plans to speak of. Do you maybe want to bring over those presents you mentioned, join us for dinner?"

"Actually, I thought I might take my kids out for supper, if you don't object. Dinner and a movie with their old man?"

"Depending on the movie you had in mind, that sounds great." She paused, softening. "I really *do* want you to have quality time with the kids. Last night was unfortunate timing."

"I appreciate that, Mackenzie. Why don't you ask the kids what films they're interested in seeing, and I'll be there in, say, half an hour?"

It took fifty-five minutes, but considering Atlanta traffic, he could be forgiven the brief delay. Rather, Kenzie could forgive it. Leslie, who'd read three chapters while waiting for her dad, didn't seem to notice. Drew, on the other hand, practically met his father at the door with a stopwatch.

Mick froze at the sight of his son. "Look at you! Lord, you've grown. Look a lot like I did at your age."

"I'm nothing like you."

Startled, Mick glanced toward Kenzie. Drew had always worshipped his father. Kenzie had tried once last spring to explain to Mick their son's growing anger, his misery that his father missed his sporting events.

"Tell him his soccer picture's in my wallet," Mick had said. "In spirit, I'm at all his games."

Nine-year-old boys could give a collective rat's ass about "spirit."

Leslie began chatting about a current movie that was based on a book her teacher had just started reading to them. "We should see that one! It's a cool story. Drew, I think you'd like it."

He hitched a shoulder. "Don't care what we see."

Mick looked baffled but didn't comment on the boy's attitude. Kenzie tried to figure out a way to pull her son aside tactfully. She understood his anger, but she'd rather he enjoy his father's company today than regret the lost opportunity later. In the end, though, she couldn't think of anything to say that wouldn't put him in an even more belligerent mood. Perhaps this was simply something father and son would have to work out for themselves.

Normally she welcomed periods of kid-free quiet; once they were gone, the silence seemed oppressive. Following her daughter's lead, Kenzie picked up a novel she'd started weeks ago, but after rereading the same paragraph three times because she kept losing her place, she conceded defeat. Then she flipped through the television channels, but Saturday-afternoon programming wasn't exactly riveting. Restless and craving comfort, she eyed the plate of chocolate chip cookies on the kitchen counter.

Don't even think about it, they'll go straight to your hips. Maybe what she should do was use the free time to exercise. In her defense, she had burned plenty of calories last night.

Heat flooded her face as she recalled the vivid details,

details that conjured longing. It had been mere hours since she'd left JT, and already she missed him. Her gaze darted across the kitchen again, this time landing on the mug she'd hand washed. The mug she'd promised to return.

She grabbed the cup and exited her apartment before she could stop herself, not even pausing to put on shoes. Barefoot, she padded across the hall and knocked once on his door.

He opened it a moment later, his immediate surprise giving way to a pleased smile. "Kenzie."

"I, uh, wanted to give this back." She held up the mug, feeling foolish.

He eyed her with affectionate cynicism. "That the only reason you're here?"

"Well, I…"

"Because it's one of a set of six, and I live alone. I do dishes enough that I don't foresee a shortage."

"Hey, I'm doing the polite thing. Besides, I live with kids. If I don't return it ASAP, you run the risk that it could get taken out by a baseball thrown indoors."

He glanced past her at the closed door of her own apartment. "Where are the kids now?"

"With their father." She slumped, unable to contain her earlier worry. If today's outing was a disaster, would Mick be even more reluctant to get involved in the children's lives? She didn't want Drew blaming himself for that down the road.

JT searched her gaze. "Why don't you come on in?"

"I can't stay." She wasn't sure why she put up the token resistance. After all, she easily could stay for the next three or four hours. It beat being at loose ends in an empty apartment, she thought as she followed him.

In the kitchen, he pulled her into his arms. "You looked like you could use a hug."

She cuddled closer, grateful for his perceptiveness. "I wonder if I'm doing a good job. There aren't enough concrete right and wrongs. Most days I just hope I'm faking it enough to fool everyone."

"I can't claim to be an expert, but from this observer's point of view, you're doing a wonderful job. The fact that you're doubting yourself because you want to do what's best for them just shows what a caring mother you are."

That earned him a kiss. How could it not, when he held her and said what she most needed to hear? But as he kissed her back, her feelings of gratitude quickly flamed into something more carnal.

When he fumbled for the buttons on her blouse, she said, "This isn't why I came over."

He rubbed a thumb over the tight peak of one breast. "Do you want to stop?"

She shuddered. "Hell, no."

"I am so glad you said that."

He scooped her up into his arms, making her feel tiny and deliciously feminine, and carried her back to his room. Last night, he'd stroked and kissed most of her, but that had been under the cover of darkness. Lying naked before him in the stark light of day was a new vulnerability, a new intimacy she hadn't intended, bringing them even closer. The first two times they'd made love, they'd been learning each other's bodies and desires. JT was a quick learner. He touched her now as if he were an expert on her every erogenous zone, knowing just how far she could tolerate his erotic teasing.

When he slid inside her, all her muscles clenched, trying to bring him even closer, hold him even tighter. As the pressure built, she moved more frantically, the ripples of pleasure becoming a crashing tsunami. She heard herself call out his name. He echoed her cry with an incoherent shout as he thrust home.

For long peaceful moments, neither of them moved—Kenzie wasn't sure she could if she wanted to. But then he shifted, rolling off her, though his gaze was still locked with hers.

"Kenzie. I…" He glanced down, then straightened suddenly, going pale. "Damn."

Her warm fuzzy feelings of afterglow cooled considerably. "What? JT, what is it?"

He stood. "The condom broke."

Chapter Fifteen

People mentioned awkward mornings-after. Kenzie had never heard the protocol for a hellishly awkward "later…that same afternoon."

She and JT had both cleaned up and dressed, yet part of her felt painfully exposed. He looked so angry. She realized the emotion was directed at the defective prophylactic, but that didn't quite stop her from feeling hurt.

"I'm sure it will be okay," she said from the middle of his living room. "I, ah, have pretty regular cycles, and it's not the right time."

He stood at the same window where they'd cuddled that morning, seeming an entirely different man than the one who'd brought her coffee. "I don't ever want to get a woman pregnant. I'm not sure I could live through that again. I know—rationally, I know—that thousands of women have healthy babies every day. But Holly didn't. I killed her."

"JT, no." Kenzie was horrified by the naked blame in his tone. While fatal labor complications had become mercifully rare, they occasionally happened. "What happened to her was a tragedy, but no one's fault."

"That's what the doctors said, too." Still not looking at her, he shivered. "I can't go through any of that again. Not just the labor or the pregnancy but all of it. Falling in l—" His voice broke.

Human compassion would have been enough to motivate Kenzie toward him even if she barely knew him. Now that she was familiar with him in the most personal of ways, seeing the pain on his face was like a knife in the stomach. She wanted so badly to embrace him and somehow absorb his suffering. Yet he moved away just as she reached him, his expression one of subtle panic.

"I can't. Don't you see that, Kenzie? I've been letting myself grow attached to you because I thought it was safe. You'll be gone soon. It won't be like when Holly was ripped away. I *know* you're leaving. And it's really not the same thing, because she was my wife and I loved her. You were just going to be... I don't know what. I'm a jackass. I persuaded myself that I wasn't falling for you, but it's not true. I can't let that happen again." He took a shaky breath. "Losing her may not have killed me, but there were plenty of days when I wished it had."

"You plan to never love again?" It struck Kenzie as unbearably sad, even though she'd clung to the same safety net he had—her leaving in a few weeks would help them part ways naturally, giving him little chance to complicate her and the kids' life.

"I was lucky enough to have those years with Holly." His face softened as he added, "And lucky enough to have this weekend with you. That's far more than some men ever get."

She opened her mouth to protest his denying himself a chance to be happy, but what could she possibly say? While she'd like to think fate would never be cruel enough to take someone away from JT again, there were no guarantees. He had so much to offer a woman, but she understood his self-protective instinct. More than she cared to.

"If you don't mind, until we move, I'll still let Drew come over and paint with you. But it's probably best if I don't…see you. Alone, I mean."

"Probably," he echoed in morose agreement.

"Goodbye, JT."

He didn't answer. When she let herself out of the apartment, he was still standing fixed in place, his posture one of dejected solitude. She told herself that he'd recover once she moved away, find a happy medium of painting and spending time with friends without getting too involved with any one person. But she knew his expression of naked loneliness would haunt her for many nights to come.

Especially when she was lying awake and missing him, battling her own lonely heart.

"SO." ANN HANDED her sister a plate of burgers fresh off the grill. They were taking them inside to stick on buns for the kids while Forrest started the next round. Meanwhile, Drew and Leslie chased each other through the lush backyard. "I waited all week to hear from you in the vain hope that baby-sitting the kids would earn me some deets."

"'Deets'?" Kenzie laughed. "You've been hanging around too much with my daughter."

"Details, woman! Spill the details about JT."

The plate wobbled in Kenzie's hands, and only Ann's reflexes kept the burgers from becoming lawn ornaments.

"Sorry." Kenzie bit her lip, scolding herself for her over-reaction. So Ann had mentioned JT—big deal; Drew had been talking about him all week. Even though the boy had mastered the right terminology, he persisted in teasing JT about being his mental rather than his mentor. JT had given Drew an actual canvas to paint on, and the results now hung in the boy's room.

Even Leslie had been impressed with her brother's efforts. "Who knew he had talents beyond soccer and creating clutter?" she'd asked, still a touch bitter that no one was helping to develop *her* artistic abilities.

Ann didn't say anything until they were inside, safely out of anyone else's earshot. "Are you okay? I noticed you sounded tense on the phone this week, but I thought that was the weirdness of Mick being in town."

"No, for the kids' sake, I'm glad Mick was here." Although she hoped it wasn't a case of too little, too late. He had indeed taken them to dinner and a movie, but Drew complained that the man had spent half the meal on his cell phone with newly recruited clients. "He's supposed to come back the week we close on the new house, hang out with the kids while I take care of things."

Ann scowled. "You ask me, you end up taking care of way too much. I'd love to see you with a guy who could take care of you for a change."

"Honestly, I'm not looking for that." Kenzie opened the refrigerator, grabbing the mustard and ketchup while Ann sliced tomatoes. "I'm okay taking care of myself. Less chance for disappointment."

"You sound cynical."

"No, just practical. See? I'm learning in my old age."

"But what about the yummy artist? Where does he fit in with practicality?"

"He doesn't." Kenzie sighed wistfully. "We both came to that conclusion last Sunday. I'm about to move out of the apartment complex, you know."

"Yeah, but you won't be living that far apart. If you really wanted to date—"

"That's just it—we don't."

"I saw the way you two looked at each other! You like him. And he's surprisingly good with the kids. Did I mention yummy? Is it that you don't want the same things?"

Actually, they did want the same thing: security. Kenzie needed stability for herself and her kids, and JT was desperately trying to safeguard himself against possible hurts.

"Ann, he's just now returning to his life and career after getting over his wife. He doesn't plan to ever really get involved with anyone else, but if he does…well, he's going to need someone with a lot of patience, a lot of extra time and TLC. Meanwhile, I have two kids, one of whom is increasingly angry and confused and in need of a lot of extra attention himself. JT's great. I wish him well, but trust me, there's no future for the two of us."

Ann thought this over, staring intently at the cutting board. "What about a present?"

"I don't follow."

"What if, instead of obsessing about the possible future or dwelling on the hurts of your past, you two just concentrated on the present? Being happy today. You both deserve that much."

"Live for today?" Kenzie shot her sister a gently teasing grin. "What kind of radical thinking is that? What happened to carefully planning ahead? That's what got you where you are now."

"Yes and no. Forrest and I spent a lot of time preparing, planning, strategizing ways for him to get ahead at the college, when the best time to have a baby might be. Sure, most of our organizing has paid off, but somewhere along the way we

forgot to enjoy the here and now. Forgot to enjoy each other."
Her cheeks flushed a rosy pink. "We're working hard to make
the time to do that."

"And no one's happier about that than me—"

"Especially since you got your apartment back." Ann
smirked.

"No comment."

Just then, a rap at the sliding glass door drew their attention. Kenzie's son stood on the other side. When he saw that
he had his mom's eye, he slapped a hand to his forehead and
pantomimed being dizzy and weak from hunger, eventually
"passing out" on Ann's porch.

Ann laughed. "Think he's trying to tell us something?"

"Let's get the burgers that are ready outside before rioting
begins." She lifted two paper plates and headed for the door.

"Kenzie?" Her sister's voice stalled her. "We don't have to
keep talking about it, especially not with the kids around, but
will you think about what I said?"

"Sure." It was an easy promise to make. After all, she'd
thought about JT and the way he made her feel every day since
she'd walked out of his apartment.

A better question than would she think about him was how
did she go about forgetting him?

AT THE HEAVY FOOTFALLS behind her, Kenzie's heart sank. She
kept her eyes on the lit elevator button, hoping for the best.
Even though she'd heard the door open at the far end of the
hall, that didn't necessarily mean JT was approaching. Maybe
it was Sean or another acquaintance…. But by the time the
man stopped behind her, she was already reacting to the subtle
scent of his cologne and the familiar warmth of his body.

"Hey," he said softly.

Curse her laziness; she'd been doing a great job of avoiding her neighbor, and if she'd only taken the stairs instead of waiting around for the elevator, she could have spared herself this encounter.

"Hi." She gave him a feeble smile over her shoulder. Even that one brief glance shredded her willpower. He looked fantastic. More than anything, she wanted to reach out and touch him. Hold him and ask how he was doing, kiss him and let him know how much his continued tutoring meant to her son.

She felt so on edge that she almost jumped at the sound of the *ding*. They filed into the elevator together, and she couldn't help thinking of the night they'd returned from their gallery date, when JT had grabbed her the second the doors closed and they'd spent the duration of the brief trip locked in each other's arms.

Her breath quickened.

"You okay?" JT frowned. "I didn't think you were claustrophobic."

"I'm fine. Just…a lot on my mind. Getting ready for the move and all." With the closing next Tuesday, she had taken this afternoon off work for the final walk-through of the house. It was a routine check to verify that everything she and the sellers had agreed on after the inspection had been addressed, and that no undisclosed last-minute damage had occurred to the property.

JT nodded. "Drew mentioned that you guys have started packing. Or, more specifically, that you've started assembling boxes and have been on his case about packing."

She lifted an eyebrow. "I—*whoa*, what was that?"

The elevator had jerked to a halt with some kind of screeching metal-on-metal sound.

"Good question." After a second, he added, "I think we might be stuck."

"What? No!" She heard the panicky note in her own voice. "I—I have a scheduled walk-through I have to get to." More to the point, being trapped in a small space with JT was— *heavenly*—her idea of hell.

"Hang on." He hit an intercom button labeled Emergency. "Hello? Anybody out there? This is Jonathan Trelauney. We're stuck in the elevator."

A moment passed, then there was the crackle of static. "JT?" Mr. C.'s voice had never sounded so good. "Don't you worry, I'll check out the problem and see if we can get you going again in a jiffy."

If he could manage it in the next five minutes, Kenzie thought wildly, she'd send him an enormous gift basket as a goodbye.

"Great, Kenzie and I would appreciate it."

"She in there, too?" Mr. C. asked. "When do your kids get home from school, hon? I can have Mrs. Sanchez meet them in the lobby and take them to her apartment if you're still in there."

It made Kenzie smile to have someone else worry about her children. "Thanks, Mr. C.," she called past JT's shoulder, "but Alicia's staying with them this afternoon anyway, because I have an errand to run. Besides, they won't be here for another hour. We'll be out by then, right?"

That was answered with silence. Then an upbeat, "I'll do my best."

Gulp. She couldn't handle being in this elevator with JT for sixty minutes—not without losing her mind, entertaining some seriously adult fantasies or both. She sat against the back wall of the elevator.

JT leaned against the short wall to her left. "If this were a movie, we'd probably bounce up and down to get the elevator moving again."

She was so not bouncing up and down in front of JT.

"Or we'd try the trapdoor on the elevator ceiling," he continued. "That's always a popular escape route in cinema."

She smiled. "I didn't realize you were such a film buff."

"Only recently. I had some friends in college who did indie movies that I supported, but I haven't paid attention to what was in theaters in years. Earlier this summer I went through a period of insomnia and started catching a lot of stuff on cable. Old black-and-white movies, new blockbusters, action flicks…marathons of makeover shows," he admitted sheepishly.

A guffaw escaped her. "Really? You and Leslie could watch them together. That's her favorite television." It had been a stupid thing to say, of course. As of next week, Leslie and Drew wouldn't see JT anymore. *And neither will I.*

She wasn't moving to the far side of the moon, but, in this case, it might as well be. If she and JT were different people committed to trying to make a relationship work, it would be worth the traffic and distance, fitting him between the kids and getting settled in their new home and community. But the last time she'd been alone with this man, he'd point-blank told her that he was looking forward to her being gone, that he just wasn't ready to share his heart.

She fell silent, but it wasn't a relaxed silence. Half the time, she could feel his gaze on her; the other half, he was trying too hard not to look at her. But aside from each other, there wasn't much else to occupy their interest inside the elevator. She read and reread the inspection notice and safety code information. Finally she realized she did have something to say—it was just painfully embarrassing to figure out how.

"JT? I thought, in case it was something you were worried about, that you should know I…" *Spit it out. The man's seen you naked, for crying out loud.* Strangely, that thought didn't soothe her. "Last week, well, I'm definitely not pregnant."

He blinked at her, as if first trying to figure out what she was talking about, then nodding vigorously. "Oh. Good. Thanks for, um, letting me know."

"You betcha." This felt like the most absurd conversation she'd ever had. And she'd spent entire days with chatty twins. "Would it be obnoxious of us to check back with Mr. C. and find out what's taking so long?"

"I just hope he doesn't mention our predicament to Mrs. Sanchez," JT grumbled. "She'd try to talk him into some crazed notion of not rescuing us, so we could have more time together. She brought over dinner last Friday and chewed my ear off about letting you leave."

"'Letting me'?" As an independent woman, Kenzie didn't know if she should be appalled or amused.

"I know, I know. She harbors some old-fashioned idea about how I'm supposed to stop you from following your own path by declaring my—" He broke off suddenly, clearing his throat. "She's a meddling busybody."

"But you love her anyway."

He looked Kenzie in the eye. "Against my better judgment, yeah, I do."

A lump of emotion swelled up in her throat, making it momentarily impossible for her to speak. Which was probably just as well. Now that she and JT were safely platonic again, why admit anything she might regret later? *Then again,* an internal imp demanded, *you move next week, so what do you have to lose by speaking up now?*

"I do have my own path to follow," she told him. "But I'll always be glad about the side detour to Peachy Acres. I…I've come to care about you a lot. I'll miss you. All three of us will miss you."

He bent forward to grab her hand and squeeze it. She held on as tightly as she could.

Then Mr. C.'s voice boomed through the intercom. "Okay, folks, the bad news is we can't get the elevator started again right now. So we're going to pry open the doors and pull you out. You've stopped just below the second floor. We'll help you out and let you take the stairs down."

Kenzie stood, staring at the doors that would soon open. When they did, she and JT would each go their own way.

JT rose, too, reaching for the back pocket of his jeans. He pulled out a worn leather wallet. The business card he handed her was a plain white rectangle, but each line of information, JONATHAN TRELAUNEY, ARTIST along with his phone number and e-mail address, were printed in a different font and color.

"You are one of the most capable people I've ever met," he said. "For months, I've been trying to figure out how to best take care of myself, and you're single-handedly taking care of a family of three, along with miscellaneous relatives who have problems of their own and some crazy guy who lives across the hall."

She laughed at that. "I'm not sure my sister qualifies as 'miscellaneous' or that I've done anything for you. Quite the reverse, actually."

"We'll just agree to disagree about that. As capable as you are, I doubt you need others often, but if you ever need anything…"

"Thank you." Touched, she closed her fingers over the card.

Outside, she could hear Mr. C. and someone else working to pull back the doors. Lightning fast, she stretched up one last time and pressed a final kiss to JT's lips. Then she sprang back. Moments later, Mr. C. and the building's college student managed to get the doors far enough open that Kenzie thought she'd just be able to squeeze through.

"You go on ahead," JT said chivalrously. "You have that house inspection. I won't be able to make it through something that narrow, but I'm in no hurry."

He went down on one knee in front of the opening, letting her use the other leg for a boost. Mr. C. and the younger man reached down and helped pull her through. Once free of the elevator, she thanked all three of them and hurried to the stairwell.

She couldn't help thinking of how she'd first met JT here. As he'd helped her pick up her slightly muddied belongings and decapitated panda bear, his expression unsmiling and his sheer size imposing, she never could have imagined the warm, caring man who would become an accidental but important part of her and the children's lives. At the bottom stair, she glanced back up, but she wasn't sure why. After all, there was nothing to see here and she had someplace to be.

Her Perfect House and pragmatically planned future awaited.

Chapter Sixteen

"Mom? Earth to Mom?" Drew snapped his fingers, looking across the kitchen table at Leslie. "What's that word you used the other day? Something about cat comas?"

After a second's thought, Leslie was able to translate. "Catatonic."

"Yeah. I think she's that," he said. "Maybe Alicia should have stayed to look after us tonight. Mom may have been turned into a pod person."

Kenzie set her fork down on her plate and gazed at her son. Between discussing stories with his sister and JT's artistic influence, Drew's imagination seemed to be taking on a life of its own lately. "I am not a pod person. I was thinking about the house."

"Is it as gorgeous as you remember?" Leslie asked dreamily.

"Um…" Was it? She'd had a weird vibe during her walk-through this afternoon. The front yard looked majestic, but she'd suddenly panicked over not only the monthly check she'd have to write for the modest acreage, but the upkeep required. In the gleaming, spacious kitchen with its modern flat-top stove, she'd had the sense that the room seemed…a little sterile and without personality. She glanced up from her kitchen table now, enjoying the comfy warmth of the place. They weren't living in a mansion, but they were living well within their means. *You're just having last-minute cold feet. Perfectly normal.*

But what if next week the cold feet became buyer's remorse, and it was too late to do anything about it?

"Oh, who wants to hear about the house?" Drew said impatiently. "We'll be there soon and can look at it as much as we want. *I* wanted to tell Mom about what happened at school today."

Pride filled Kenzie. Over the past two weeks, Drew had become more and more engaged. He had a small group of friends he mentioned regularly, and he'd fallen into the habit of sharing weird facts he'd learned in social studies or science. "What happened?"

"First, I got a B on that test yesterday, and it was *really* hard, too. But also, Mrs. Frazer talked about how we're going to have fine-arts week in November, and I told her I knew a local artist who's famous and everything. I don't think she believed me at first, but she's heard of JT. She was impressed! I told her JT would come talk to our class, and now I'm, like, her favorite kid. She asked me to bring in one of the paintings I've done to discuss during art week."

Kenzie's mind went blank. On the one hand, it was thrilling for a mother to have her son so enthusiastic about school, and she didn't want to dampen what he was feeling right now. On the other, he couldn't just go around volunteering adults—especially not *that* adult—for class events. She'd expected the move to provide a clean break between JT and her family. It was surprising to realize it might be more complicated than that.

"Mom?" he pressed. "Did you hear what I said?"

"Absolutely, and great job getting that B! But, sweetheart, we don't know if JT will be available to come to your classroom."

"I'll ask him tonight," Drew said matter-of-factly. "I'm supposed to go over there after dinner. I'm sure he won't mind."

"Maybe not, but… You know we won't be seeing much of JT after we move, right?"

"I've been thinking about that. Couldn't I still come and paint with him after school? You could just drive over and get me, then take me home."

"That will take forever," Leslie complained. "I don't want to be stuck at the house waiting for you guys to come home at night."

"Drew, you told me he was working on a new abstract series. That will probably take up more of his time. And Leslie's right, it won't be convenient to slog through evening rush hour once we live in the opposite direction. Atlanta traffic is totally different from Raindrop's."

"It doesn't have to be every day," he wheedled. "Just sometimes. Can we at least ask JT about it? He likes having me around."

"I'll tell you what, let's drop that for now, but you can go ahead and ask him about November. Please don't be disappointed or angry if he says no."

"I won't, but I'm sure he'll say yes! JT's the type of guy you can count on." Drew carried his empty plate to the sink. "I'm going over to decide what to do for art week. Knowing Mrs. Frazer, she'll want a painting that manages a 'dialogue' or something. I think she's a little nuts."

Kenzie could empathize. Her world wasn't making as much sense these days, either.

AS HAD BECOME THEIR HABIT, JT and Drew went up to the roof to work. Even if the kid weren't moving away, they wouldn't be able to continue their lessons in the evenings, not now that daylight saving had kicked in and the sky darkened much earlier with the approaching winter.

This would probably be the last time Drew came over. It was funny how JT had started this as a way to help the boy— or, more accurately, the boy's blue-eyed mother—yet he felt as if he'd really gained something indefinable and special. Maybe he'd talk to Sean about trying to set up some part-time teaching gigs, or even once-a-month free classes for kids at their gallery.

Drew had been nervous when he first arrived tonight, but once he'd asked about his elementary school's upcoming art week and was reassured JT didn't mind attending, he'd calmed down and turned his attention to his painting.

It was JT who was now nervously obsessing over the November appearance and couldn't focus on his work. Was the school's art week something that parents attended, too? Would he see Kenzie there? Both she and Drew had mentioned Mick's attempts to be in Atlanta more, so maybe *he'd* show up, as well. For the kid's sake, JT hoped so.

He hadn't been able to get Kenzie out of his mind since their interlude in the elevator earlier—or her confession of how much she'd come to care about him. It was the kind of thing he knew he wasn't brave enough to say, because those admissions led to deeper feelings, the exact opposite of the safe distance he craved. Yet even knowing that separation was safer, he'd had to fight the urge to ask Drew about Kenzie's week or how she was doing. *Or whether she's mentioned me lately.*

Pathetic. No self-respecting man would use a nine-year-old as an unwitting spy.

Glancing toward Drew, JT chuckled to himself. Nor should a self-respecting man let a nine-year-old outshine him with a better work ethic. With that thought, he turned to his palette and got down to the business of painting.

When Drew came over to say it was time for him to go, JT was so engrossed in the burgeoning creation that it took him a minute to realize the boy was speaking to him.

"That's cool," Drew said. "Does it have a title?"

"Not yet." JT stepped aside so that his protégé could take a better look.

"I think it looks like people." He studied the different colored blobs on the canvas. "These smaller ones could be kids, the bigger ones the adults. Like a family. Maybe that's what you should call it—'Picture of a Family.'"

JT raised his eyebrows; there were a lot of blobs. "That's a pretty big family."

"Like Mrs. Sanchez's. She has a lot of relatives. I think she's the red blob." Drew pointed toward a blurred sphere near the upper corner of the canvas. "I'm gonna miss her when we move."

"You'll make new friends. After all, you and Leslie didn't want to move from Raindrop, either, and you made new friends here."

"I guess." The boy looked unconvinced, but nodded anyway. "Do you want to go downstairs so I can clean my brushes, or should I just leave the stuff up here?"

"I'll clean up for both of us," JT promised. "You run along so we don't get in trouble with your mom."

Drew looked unperturbed by this possibility. "I don't think she'd ever be mad at you. She likes you too much."

JT laughed. "Your logic's flawed, son. After all, she *loves* you—does that stop her from getting mad?"

At that, Drew scooted promptly toward the door, calling a quick good-night over his shoulder.

After the boy was gone, JT continued painting until the evening grew chilly and his fingers uncomfortable. Then he took everything back to his apartment and kept on painting, ignoring the passing hours. Finally he stopped to look at what had taken shape on the canvas. A family, Drew had said. JT had grown up feeling disconnected from his own, then had violently lost the one he and Holly had formed. It was something that, deep down, he could admit he desperately wanted…but was afraid to reach for.

He looked again at the picture, a miasma of colors dominated by a rough rectangle. On top of and surrounding the rectangle were blobs of different sizes and shapes. His mouth twitched as he found himself thinking of the red splotch as Roberta—red was a good shade for her passionate temperament and spicy dishes. Maybe the white, skinny oval toward the bottom could represent grizzled Mr. C. And the bright yellow in the middle of the canvas, the unintentional sun the other shapes revolved around? Definitely Kenzie. He'd winced when she moved in, afraid she would disrupt his existence. God, he was glad she had. She'd brought with her such a brightness that…

I have a family.

The thought came out of nowhere as he glanced back to the canvas. Sean was like a brother to him, Roberta Sanchez an opinionated but favorite aunt. The people in this building had slowly taken up space in his hollow heart, none more so than the beautiful woman across the hall and her two children. What she'd said earlier today was true—he did love Mrs.

Sanchez. And he would be devastated should anything bad ever happen to Sean, yet that didn't stop JT from treasuring the man's friendship or going into business with him. Wasn't it just as possible to lose one of those people as someone he loved romantically?

It's not the same. A dull phantom pain ached in his chest. If Sean got hit on the head with an asteroid tomorrow, it would suck, but it would be different than the I've-just-been-torn-in-half mindless sorrow of losing Holly. Just as the risks of romantic love were greater, though, weren't the rewards, as well?

Did he want to be a colorless, solitary blob on his own dark canvas, or did he want to be part of a family, a returning member of the world that he painted but too seldom participated in? He didn't even have to think about the answer.

Instinct and raw emotion, the kind he'd been trying so hard not to feel, propelled him out his apartment and straight to Kenzie's door.

EVEN THOUGH IT HADN'T jostled her from sleep—she was too restless for that—a knock on the door at one in the morning was startling. Was there some kind of emergency in the building? Was her ex in town, looking for a place to crash after an event at a nightclub? The very last person she expected to find was wild-eyed JT, his hair standing on end, brightly colored smudges on his sleeveless white undershirt and jeans.

"JT? What's wrong?" She stepped out into the hall, pulling the door partially closed behind her so they didn't wake the kids.

"No, it's what's *right*." His expression was one of almost manic joy. She was still trying to decipher it when he grabbed her and kissed her passionately.

Momentary shock turned to a flame of bright arousal, her body much faster to respond than her confused mind. Heat pulsed within her, and she opened her mouth, seeking closer contact. But the insistent part of her asking *what the hell?* finally made itself heard long enough for her to pull away.

"JT, I don't understand. What—"

"I love you. Mrs. Sanchez was right. I should declare my love and try to keep you from leaving Peachy Acres. Or at least from leaving me. Don't leave me, Kenzie. I need you. You've changed my life. I still don't know if I could handle having a woman being pregnant with my baby, but my time with Drew… I always wondered if I would be a good dad and now, I think, yes. Even though my chance was taken away from me, even though my own role model wasn't— I could be a father. And I can paint again! Come see what I've just finished. Maybe I could explain it better that way than in words, but—"

"Stop!" Her head was reeling. She felt dizzy and was frantic to get off this unexpected roller coaster. She couldn't keep up with the information he was throwing at her. "I need a minute."

"I love you." He repeated it almost more to himself than to her, and her heart leaped with joy at the statement.

He loves me. Her toes curled inside her fuzzy pink socks. No. She tamped down her budding euphoria. At least one of them had to stay grounded in reality—a role with which she was too familiar.

"JT, this is insane."

He offered her a lopsided smile. "Artists usually are crazy."

Tell me something I don't know. Though he was joking, he wasn't helping his own case. "Look, you know how much I care about you, but I'm not a teenager anymore. I can't allow myself to be blindly swept off my feet. I have two kids to think of."

"I know, and they're wonderful kids. Like I was just telling you—"

"It's one in the morning! You're jubilant because you've just finished what I'm sure is a brilliant painting. You're coasting on artist endorphins or adrenaline or whatever, but that's no reason for deciding you want to be a father figure. Especially not to two children who already have one wacky dad in their lives."

JT stiffened. Her rejection was starting to sink in. "I'm not 'wacky.' It's not fair for you to automatically paint me with the same brush as Mick, if you'll pardon the expression."

Part of her wanted to agree with him, assure him that she thought he'd be a much better and selfless father. The rest of her was fleeing in blind panic and wasn't willing to stop to entertain the possibilities.

"I've already been one man's muse," she heard herself say, not liking the note of hysteria that was creeping into her tone. "You're crediting me with you being able to paint again. I don't *want* that responsibility. What happens if you get stuck, or a critic hates your latest piece? Are you going to blame me for that, maybe without even meaning to? Are you going to growl that the kids are a distraction, that none of us understand…? It's one in the morning, JT."

"I'm aware of the time." He sounded angry, but there was sheepish acknowledgment in his gaze that perhaps he'd acted too impetuously. "Could I come back tomorrow, at a more civilized hour, so that we could discuss this?"

She gripped the doorknob behind her, retreating. "I don't think that's a good idea. You yourself told me not long ago that you didn't want to fall in love."

"That's when I was arrogant enough to think I could control it, but you—"

"No, I didn't do anything. Not intentionally. We were both honest about not wanting anything long-term. I…I can't."

Rocking back on his heels, he assessed her. "You're as scared as I was. I thought you were more courageous."

"I never claimed to be."

"It's all right." His voice had gentled. "We can work through our fears together. We can—"

"There is no we!" She opened her door and turned to escape. "Goodbye, JT."

She didn't slam the door in his face, but it somehow felt like she did. Inside, she leaned against the frame, letting the tears come. *I'm doing the right thing.* He was clearly not in a rational mood, and she was making the adult choice for both of them. Just as she'd done repeatedly in her marriage. She was not going down that road again.

No matter how tempted she'd been to tell him she loved him, too.

SHE WAS GAINING A HOUSE but losing a dress size, Kenzie thought in the ladies' lounge of the lawyer's office. Lack of appetite the past few days meant that the once sharp business suit she'd chosen to wear to the house closing was hanging limply on her frame. It wasn't a good look. Still, she was about to walk into that oval conference room and sign away her life savings, so new wardrobe additions were out of the question.

After applying more lipstick, she slid the tube in her purse and checked to make sure she'd remembered all the necessary items for today—checkbook, driver's license, social-security card. She had just finished her inventory and stepped into the lushly carpeted corridor when her cell phone buzzed. Probably Ann calling to wish her luck. Or Mick rescheduling again. He'd been due to arrive last night, but had to postpone. At least he'd bothered to let her know, something he hadn't always done in the past.

"Hello?"

"Mrs. Green? This is Ms. Taylor, the school nurse. We need you to come pick up Andrew. I'm afraid he's just thrown up. There is a nasty stomach bug going around."

Oh, the poor baby. "Is he all right? Do you think I should get him to the pediatrician?"

"He's resting comfortably, no fever. I wouldn't be too alarmed, ma'am, but he definitely can't stay here with the other students."

"Of course not." She peered through the glass at the real estate agents and attorneys already seated at the mahogany table. "I'm not in an area of town where I can reach him anytime soon. And I'm supposed to be… Can I have someone else pick him up?"

"You'll have to call us personally with the name of the individual and they'll need to show photo ID in the office."

"I'll get right back to you." She disconnected, holding up an index finger at her frowning Realtor. Damn. If Mick had been able to make it, that would be a quick solution. Ann lived too far away; by the time she got Abigail all ready and into her car seat… Mrs. Sanchez was a likely possibility, if she were home this afternoon, but Kenzie didn't have the woman's number with her and would need to call information.

Or.

Peeking into her purse, she fished out the business card JT had handed her. If you ever need anything, he'd said. But what kind of woman coldly refused a man's love, then phoned him for a favor? *A mom whose pride isn't as important as her kid.*

She punched in his number, holding her breath until he answered, and cut him off in mid-hello. "It's Kenzie. I need to ask—"

"Aren't you supposed to be closing on a new house?"

"Exactly. But Drew's school just called. He threw up. Even if I walk out on the closing—"

"I can get him. Just give me directions."

Five minutes later, she'd authorized the plan for the school and was able to go into the conference room. But her mind wouldn't focus on all the contract clauses the attorney was trying to explain. *I can get him.* That had been JT's immediate reaction to her needing help. There'd been no hesitation, no snarky response.

He'd caught her so off guard the other night, when he'd rushed over to share his 1:00 a.m. epiphany, that she'd been startled and disoriented. If she hadn't been panicking, would she ever have compared him to her first husband? She cringed, recalling that she'd implied he was wacky. JT had disrupted his own comfortable solitude to be there for her and her kids. Even a nine-year-old could see that. What was it Drew had said, confident his newfound hero would want to help with art week? *JT's the type of guy you can count on.*

He sure as hell was.

"Mrs. Green?" The lawyer smiled at her, but sounded vaguely impatient. "Are you with us?"

"No. I mean, I am, but I shouldn't be. I'm sorry, a few moments ago I received a call about my son, and I…I need to be somewhere else." She stood as her agent turned to the sellers and tried to do damage control, mentioning a family emergency and rescheduling. Kenzie could barely hear the words over the buzzing in her head of thousands of lightbulbs coming on at once.

She loved JT.

She loved his artistic side, loved his big heart, evidenced by how much he'd adored his first wife and by how he'd let Kenzie and her kids into his life. And she loved how steady he was. He was *not* Mick. Maybe her first husband was going to follow through on his attempts to become a better father, maybe that would be a short-lived fiasco. Either way, she and the kids would be all right, and she had no business punishing JT for another man's failures.

The length of the red lights seemed to grow in direct contrast to her need to reach home. *Home.* That truly was what she considered Peachy Acres these days, although she imagined she could feel that way about any place where her children were and where JT was nearby.

When she reached the apartment building, she parked the car and raced to the stairwell. She wasn't taking her chances with the elevator. By the time she banged on JT's door, she was breathless.

He frowned down at her. "Kenzie? I thought you were—"

She grabbed him by the front of his shirt and simultaneously launched herself upward in a kiss that said all the things it would take too long to vocalize. For a shining second, she understood what he'd said about thinking in colors. Starbursts of light and joy exploded behind her eyes, her longing for this man obliterating anything as mundane as words. To her delight and relief, JT did not hesitate or push her away. He cradled her to him, meeting her kiss with fervent, open-mouthed abandon.

"Mom!"

Oh, dear heaven. How had she forgotten about Drew? She angled her head away from JT—not willing to let go of him, though—and saw her curious son sprawled on JT's couch beneath a quilt.

"Um...hey, honey, feeling better?" She was officially the worst mother in the world, but her son wasn't glaring.

"Well, I've managed not to yarf in JT's apartment," he said.

She could feel JT's silent laughter beneath her fingers. "That's much appreciated," he said.

Drew narrowed his eyes. "I know what you said before, Mom, but does this mean you two will be dating, after all?"

She bit her lip. "How would you feel about that, kiddo?"

Her son's face took on an exhilarated expression and he pumped his fist in the air. "Cool! Leslie is gonna be so mad that I found out first."

Kenzie took JT's hand and led him a few feet away, toward the kitchen, where she could speak quietly and not with an audience. "I am sorry about the other night."

"Don't be," he told her with a tender smile. "Some of what you said was true. It was unthinking of me to bang on your door at one in the morning. On a school night, no less. What was I expecting you to do, sweep me inside and let me make love to you with impressionable children down the hall? I was a bit out of line."

"And I was a lot out of line. I let my past build up fears about the future."

He ran a hand over her hair. "I know a little something about that. To tell you the truth, those fears are still there, but they're not as strong as what I feel for you."

Moved beyond speaking, she kissed him again, incredibly grateful that they had each found this second chance at love and happiness. All that was missing was an orchestral swell of beautiful music to make this a movie-perfect moment.

"Hey! When you guys are finished sucking face, could someone get me some ginger ale?"

Kenzie felt JT's smile against her lips and thought, *Close enough.*

Epilogue

It was a gorgeous June wedding, with Sean serving as best man and Ann, pregnant *again,* glowing in her matron-of-honor dress. Since weather delays had made it impossible for Kenzie's parents—doing humanitarian work in South America—to attend, Mr. C. had agreed to give her away. The whole of Peachy Acres turned out for the small but lovely rooftop ceremony, and Mrs. Sanchez made the wedding cake. If anyone thought it was odd for Kenzie's first husband to be among the guests, they kept it to themselves. For her part, Kenzie was thrilled that he'd honored his promise to be here and to keep the kids while she and JT went to the beach for a weekend honeymoon.

As she walked down the "aisle," she couldn't help thinking of JT's first marriage. *I promise to love him as much as you did,* she vowed to the unseen Holly, who she liked to think was here in spirit and approved.

After their honeymoon, they'd be moving to a nearby suburb. It was older than the neighborhood Kenzie had almost ended up in, but the house had character and the perfect small building in the backyard to serve as a studio for her new husband, whose recent abstract series "Family Portraits" was garnering critical acclaim. Leslie and Drew did not share in their mom's demurring that she couldn't take responsibility for his talent.

"We take full credit for inspiring him," they bragged to their friends.

As Mrs. Sanchez cut slices of cake for the happy couple, she reminded them, "I expect to see you both at the Labor Day picnic!"

"We wouldn't miss it," Kenzie promised.

The older woman raised her eyebrows. "Maybe by then, your sister won't be the only one pregnant, eh?"

"I don't know. I'm pretty happy with the two I've got." Returning to diapers and sleepless nights after a decade? Probably not. But if she and JT made that decision, she knew she had an equal partner in parenting.

For his part, JT had told her when he proposed that the possibility of her carrying his baby still terrified him, but that he was trying to let go of the fear. "After all, I received one of the biggest blessings of my life when I stopped being scared and let myself love you."

Now that love was evident on his face for all to see. "Dance with me, Mrs. Trelauney?"

"Happily." She snuggled into his arms as someone turned up the CD player. In her peripheral vision, she saw Drew waltz by with the much taller Alicia, and grinned.

"That's the smile I like to see," JT murmured.

"Good." She lowered her voice to a wicked whisper. "Because once we reach our hotel, I plan to spend a lot of time wearing that smile and not much else."

"Nude, hmm?" Her husband matched her teasing tone. "Maybe now would be a good time to talk to you about a new series of paintings I'm thinking of...."

* * * * *

*We hope you're enjoying crisscrossing the country,
reading the books in*
THE STATE OF PARENTHOOD *miniseries.*
*It's time to go west again, to a small farming community
in Colorado's Rocky Mountains. Here you will meet
Leah Williams, a midwife who has volunteered to carry
her sister's child—only when the sister finds herself
unexpectedly pregnant she leaves Leah, literally,*
HOLDING THE BABY.
*Things are further complicated by the fact that the donor,
Mark Logan, wants to be involved in his child's life.*

Read on for an excerpt from Margot Early's
HOLDING THE BABY,
*coming October 2008,
only from Harlequin American Romance.*

Chapter One

Paonia, Colorado

"I'm pregnant," Ellen announced gleefully.

"You're what?" Not the reaction Ellen was probably looking for, Leah Williams thought. That her younger half sister, thirty-two, and happily married for six years, was carrying a longed-for child should have been great news. As it was, Leah absently poured orange juice, intended for four-year-old Mary Grace's cup, into her bowl of muesli.

"Mom!"

"Oh, sh— Sorry. I'll eat it. Maybe I can pour it… Darling, just a minute."

The life inside Leah's abdomen gave a kick, as if the baby could sense the turmoil Ellen's words had caused.

"So we'll be pregnant together," Ellen continued, "and we'll have babies at about the same time. Mine's due December first. I think. Anyhow, our kids will be cousins and really close in age…."

I never planned on keeping this baby. This was your baby, Ellen.

"Ellen, hang on. I need to deal with cereal." She put down

the phone. Ellen was pregnant. How was Ellen pregnant? And what was supposed to happen to the baby—Ellen's baby, for crying out loud—that Leah was carrying?

Of course, Ellen had made *her* thoughts clear: Leah would keep the baby. Leah was having a hard time organizing her own thoughts.

She picked up the phone and said, "Mary Grace, I'm going in the other room for a minute."

Her daughter, who had Sam's hay-colored hair and Leah's dark eyes, nodded without looking up from her bowl. She ate with deliberation, as she did everything.

Leah stared out the window. The two acres of peach orchards on which the small historic farmhouse sat had been Sam's promised land. Leah loved the little three-bedroom house, loved to gaze out over the fertile valley at the snow-draped mountains.

Giving herself a shake, she put the phone to her ear.

First thing first. Though she wasn't sure what should come first.

She spoke to her sister. "You're thinking…I'll just keep this baby."

"Well, it's up to you," Ellen said. "But I thought you'd want to."

Leah sighed and walked back over to the windows that fronted the tiny living room. Gazing out at mountains far to the north, she asked, "How did you come to be pregnant?"

Ellen's husband, River, was a Desert Storm veteran. After leaving the military, he'd changed his name and taken up organic farming. Then he'd met Ellen, and ever since, they'd been trying for a pregnancy. After several months and no baby, they'd figured that they were, as a couple, infertile, and, unwilling to go to a fertility clinic, they'd asked Leah to have a child for them, the sperm to be provided by River's half brother, Mark.

Leah had been insistent that the proposed conception take place at a proper facility, using the technology she knew her sister and River found so distasteful. But she'd drawn the line at having a baby the natural way with Mark Logan!

River and Ellen, talked through every step of the process and reassured that no fertility drugs, for instance, would be used, had finally agreed that the insemination could take place in the office of a nearby midwife, Cassandra Warner.

"You're pregnant," Leah repeated. "With River's child."

"Yes. Of course." Ellen paused. "You *will* be our midwife, won't you?"

"Yes," said Leah. She was ready to put down the phone and be alone and think—or maybe just scream. Granted, Ellen hadn't *planned* this. Ellen and River had believed that they couldn't conceive a child together. Nonetheless, the situation seemed so typical. Ellen was flighty and unreliable, and Leah had allowed herself to be persuaded to conceive and carry a child to give to her sister and River. And now this.

She had to get off the phone. But there was still one question to ask, because the child she carried... Well, the baby had another biological parent. "Does Mark know?"

There was a pause. "I hadn't thought to let him know. I guess I should, because River and I won't be the parents of your baby. You will be. I'll call him. Right now. Go back to Mary Grace."

Click.

Leah sank onto an antique love seat by the window. Once again her gaze was drawn to the distant mountains. Mark Logan.

She'd known him for years, though just as an acquaintance. Women throughout the San Juan Mountains and north along

Colorado's western slope swore he was like a brother to them, that he was the best guy there was. Men respected him. And everyone agreed that he was the most capable mountaineer and backcountry guide in the area.

Leah found him abrasive. For whatever reason, she'd never felt comfortable in his presence. In any case, he'd never gone out of his way to secure her good opinion. He had been Ellen's choice as a father for the child Leah now carried. Ellen's and River's. Leah definitely would have picked someone else. But she'd gone along with the baby project because Ellen and River had been desperate, and Leah had wanted to give this to her sister.

Well, it could be worse. Mark could come to Paonia and fight her over this child. Luckily for her, that wasn't going to happen. After having donated sperm to this project, he'd left and hadn't looked back. He would leave the hard decisions to her.

Now, she must make them.

Chapter 1

October
New York City

Nicole Masters was sitting cross-legged on her sofa while a cold autumn rain peppered the windows of her fourth-floor apartment. She was poking at the ice cream in her bowl and trying not to be in a mood.

Six weeks ago, a simple trip to her neighborhood pharmacy had turned into a nightmare. She'd walked into the middle of a robbery. She never even saw the man who shot her in the head and left her for dead. She'd survived, but some of her senses had not. She was dealing with short-term memory loss and a tendency to stagger. Even though she'd been told the problems were most likely temporary, she waged a daily battle with depression.

Her parents had been killed in a car wreck when she was twenty-one. And except for a few friends—and most recently her boyfriend, Dominic Tucci, who lived in the apartment right above hers, she was alone. Her doctor kept reminding her that she should be grateful to be alive, and on one level she knew he was right. But he wasn't living in her shoes.

If she'd been anywhere else but at that pharmacy when the robbery happened, she wouldn't have died twice on the way to the hospital. Instead of being grateful that she'd survived, she couldn't stop thinking of what she'd lost.

But that wasn't the end of her troubles. On top of everything else, something strange was happening inside her head. She'd begun to hear odd things: sounds, not voices—at least, she didn't think it was voices. It was more like the distant noise of rapids—a rush of wind and water inside her head that, when it came, blocked out everything around her. It didn't happen often, but when it did, it was frightening, and it was driving her crazy.

The blank moments, which is what she called them, even had a rhythm. First there came that sound, then a cold sweat, then panic with no reason. Part of her feared it was the beginning of an emotional breakdown. And part of her feared it wasn't—that it was going to turn out to be a permanent souvenir of her resurrection.

Frustrated with herself and the situation as it stood, she upped the sound on the TV remote. But instead of *Wheel of Fortune,* an announcer broke in with a special bulletin.

"This just in. Police are on the scene of a kidnapping that occurred only hours ago at The Dakota. Molly Dane, the six-year-old daughter of one of Hollywood's block-buster stars, Lyla Dane, was taken by force from the family apartment. At this time they have yet to receive a ransom demand. The housekeeper was seriously injured during the abduction, and is, at the present time, in surgery. Police are hoping to be able to talk to her once she regains consciousness. In the meantime, we are going now to a press conference with Lyla Dane."

Horrified, Nicole stilled as the cameras went live to where the actress was speaking before a bank of microphones. The shock and terror in Lyla Dane's voice were physically painful to watch. But even though Nicole kept upping the volume, the sound continued to fade.

Just when she was beginning to think something was wrong with her set, the broadcast suddenly switched from the Dane press conference to what appeared to be footage of the kidnapping, beginning with footage from inside the apartment.

When the front door suddenly flew back against the wall and four men rushed in, Nicole gasped. Horrified, she quickly realized that this must have been caught on a security camera inside the Dane apartment.

As Nicole continued to watch, a small Asian woman, who she guessed was the maid, rushed forward in an effort to keep them out. When one of the men hit her in the face with his gun, Nicole moaned. The violence was too reminiscent of what she'd lived through. Sick to her stomach, she fisted her hands against her belly, wishing it was over, but unable to tear her gaze away.

When the maid dropped to the carpet, the same man followed with a vicious kick to the little woman's midsection that lifted her off the floor.

"Oh, my God," Nicole said. When blood began to pool beneath the maid's head, she started to cry.

As the tape played on, the four men split up in different directions. The camera caught one running down a long marble hallway, then disappearing into a room. Moments later he reappeared, carrying a little girl, who Nicole assumed was Molly Dane. The child was wearing a pair of red pants and a white turtleneck sweater, and her hair was partially blocking her abductor's face as he carried her down the hall. She was kicking and screaming in his arms, and when he slapped her, it elicited an agonized scream that brought the other three running. Nicole watched in horror as one of them ran up and put his hand over Molly's face. Seconds later, she went limp.

One moment they were in the foyer, then they were gone.

Nicole jumped to her feet, then staggered drunkenly. The bowl of ice cream she'd absentmindedly placed in her lap shattered at her feet, splattering glass and melting ice cream everywhere.

The picture on the screen abruptly switched from the kidnapping to what Nicole assumed was a rerun of Lyla Dane's plea for her daughter's safe return, but she was numb.

Before she could think what to do next, the doorbell rang. Startled by the unexpected sound, she shakily swiped at the tears and took a step forward. She didn't feel the glass shards piercing her feet until she took the second step. At that point, sharp pains shot through her foot. She gasped, then looked down in confusion. Her legs looked as if she'd been running through mud, and she was standing in broken glass and ice cream, while a thin ribbon of blood seeped out from beneath her toes.

"Oh, no," Nicole mumbled, then stifled a second moan of pain.

The doorbell rang again. She shivered, then clutched her head in confusion.

"Just a minute!" she yelled, then tried to sidestep the rest of the debris as she hobbled to the door.

When she looked through the peephole in the door, she didn't know whether to be relieved or regretful.

It was Dominic, and as usual, she was a mess.

Nicole smiled a little self-consciously as she opened the door to let him in. "I just don't know what's happening to me. I think I'm losing my mind."

"Hey, don't talk about my woman like that."

Nicole rode the surge of delight his words brought. "So I'm still your woman?"

Dominic lowered his head.

Their lips met.

The kiss proceeded.

Slowly.

Thoroughly.

* * * * *

Be sure to look for the AFTERSHOCK *anthology next month, as well as other exciting paranormal stories from Silhouette Nocturne.*
Available in October wherever books are sold.

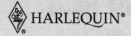

REQUEST YOUR FREE BOOKS!

2 FREE NOVELS PLUS 2
FREE GIFTS!

American ★ Romance®

Heart, Home & Happiness!

YES! Please send me 2 FREE Harlequin American Romance® novels and my 2 FREE gifts (gifts are worth about $10). After receiving them, if I don't wish to receive any more books, I can return the shipping statement marked "cancel." If I don't cancel, I will receive 4 brand-new novels every month and be billed just $4.24 per book in the U.S. or $4.99 per book in Canada, plus 25¢ shipping and handling per book and applicable taxes, if any*. That's a savings of close to 15% off the cover price! I understand that accepting the 2 free books and gifts places me under no obligation to buy anything. I can always return a shipment and cancel at any time. Even if I never buy another book from Harlequin, the two free books and gifts are mine to keep forever.

154 HDN EEZK 354 HDN EEZV

Name _____ (PLEASE PRINT)

Address _____ Apt. #

City _____ State/Prov. _____ Zip/Postal Code

Signature (if under 18, a parent or guardian must sign)

Mail to the **Harlequin Reader Service:**
IN U.S.A.: P.O. Box 1867, Buffalo, NY 14240-1867
IN CANADA: P.O. Box 609, Fort Erie, Ontario L2A 5X3

Not valid to current subscribers of Harlequin American Romance books.

Want to try two free books from another line?
Call 1-800-873-8635 or visit www.morefreebooks.com.

* Terms and prices subject to change without notice. N.Y. residents add applicable sales tax. Canadian residents will be charged applicable provincial taxes and GST. Offer not valid in Quebec. This offer is limited to one order per household. All orders subject to approval. Credit or debit balances in a customer's account(s) may be offset by any other outstanding balance owed by or to the customer. Please allow 4 to 6 weeks for delivery. Offer available while quantities last.

Your Privacy: Harlequin is committed to protecting your privacy. Our Privacy Policy is available online at www.eHarlequin.com or upon request from the Reader Service. From time to time we make our lists of customers available to reputable third parties who may have a product or service of interest to you. If you would prefer we not share your name and address, please check here. ☐

HAR08R